Moonshadows- And Other Sho

Foreword.

This is a collection of seven of my short stories. Some I wrote quite a while ago and some recently. Obviously, they can be read in any order but I thought I would give you a brief description of each – to help you decide.

1. **Moonshadows.** This is the story of a lonely man who receives a mysterious caller on the first night of each full moon. This strange visitor takes him into the realm of the "Shadow World" and shows him the denizens of that nighttime place.

2. **The Seven Chambers.** This is a tale told by the Bard, Mallon to villagers around a blazing, communal campfire. It is set in a mythical time when heroes and wizards still walked the earth. A reluctant adventurer has to face tests and challenges in **The Seven Chambers** in order to obtain a legendary sword of power, with which to exact vengeance and save his people and his lady-love.

3. **The Gauntlet.** The account of a spectacular but deadly sporting event, set in a somewhat dystopian future.

4. **Killer Krew.** A gang of sadistic thrill killers, carry out a series of brutal murders, involving rape and torture. In this story, they stalk a new victim.

5. **The Munagwyn.** There are Goblins living under the hill. This is my first encounter with **The Munagwyn,** who appear, in a more refined form in my books, **"Wolf-Warrior"** and **"The Saga of King Erk Greenhand,"**

6. **KILL THEM ALL!.** Not one for the squeamish. A dark tale of malevolent possession – or the story of a psychotic and deranged murderer – or maybe even both. You decide.

7. **The Ghost of Riverside Day Centre.** I finish with a true account of a series of supernatural experiences I had back in the 1970s. It all happened just as I describe it here.

Edward G. Lavery.

Moonshadows.

The room dimmed, as I loaded more coal onto the fire. Outside, the wind was growing in strength, making the surrounding trees creak and moan in protest. The aged sinews of my modest little cottage groaned in sympathy and rain beat a sporadic tattoo against the windows. I poured another brandy and settled back into my well-worn and beloved fireside chair. Would he come? It was almost midnight. I sipped brandy and waited. The newly laid coal was catching now and the firelight began to dance and flicker on the walls of the living room, as the flames grew higher. I savoured the moment. There is something profoundly comforting about sitting by the light of an open fire, glass in hand, listening to the wind and the rain performing in concert outside your walls. I imagined the clouds racing overhead in the wind. Shining above them was the full-moon, though no hint of it showed below. I wondered if that would be a problem. Would it stop him coming? On the two previous visits, the full-moon had been shining clear and bright. There was nothing to do but wait.

And so I waited, sipping brandy and musing on nothing in particular. The wind blew and the rain rattled. On the wall, my favourite clock ticked loudly and regularly, like something from an old Agatha Christie movie. Occasionally, the fire hissed or shifted, as it settled more comfortably in the hearth. He wasn't coming. Earlier, I had wondered how I would feel if he didn't arrive. Would I be disappointed or relieved? As it happened, I was too relaxed and dreamy to care. I just nestled further into the comforting caress of my armchair and let myself drift off to sleep. From time to time, I was drowsily aware of my surroundings and at some point my old black and white cat, Trouble, had got himself onto my lap and curled up for the night. More by habit than intention, I scratched gently at the fur on the back of his neck and he purred lazily in response.

I honestly couldn't say for certain when I actually became aware. It wasn't anything sudden or dramatic. The wind and rain had evidently stopped and the room was in silence. Even my Agatha Christie ticking had stopped, although its absence took a minute or two to register. Without really realizing it, my eyes had kind of drifted open and I was staring at the ceiling. I idly contemplated the cracks and damp patches that showed quite clearly in the silvery light. I think that was when it sunk in. He was here! I sat up groggily and tried to gather my wits. In so doing, I disturbed Trouble and he left my lap for the floor. Purring loudly, it always reminded me of a pneumatic drill, he rubbed himself against my leg, while I stroked his head, just the way he liked. Although I was now aware of my visitor, I couldn't take my eyes from Trouble, as he wandered casually to the cat-flap. He looked back once and then pushed through. My vision blurred for a moment and a lump came to my throat, at the sudden realization I would never see him again.

"It's time."

His voice drew me back to the moment and I blurted out some semi-coherent acknowledgement, as I looked towards him for the first time that night. The unearthly silence that had heralded his arrival, was giving away to an even more unearthly and strangely harmonic chorus of sighs and whispers. Somewhere, at an indefinable distance, something was singing. Other voices faded in and out, weaving complex patterns of disturbing yet alluring rhythms and harmonies with the first. He stood in the shadows at the far side of the fireplace, looking steadily towards me, with one hand resting on the mantle. "Well?" It was as much a command as a question. I nodded assent and walked somewhat shakily to the door, pausing only to pull on my coat and pick up my favourite walking stick. He followed on, shrouded in his black hooded cloak and leaning lightly on his staff. Outside, the moonlight illuminated my garden and the surrounding countryside with a glowing silver light – despite the fact that overhead clouds still formed an almost unbroken barrier and the rain still whipped down, at the mercy of a capricious wind.

We turned right and made our way on the path, by way of my strawberry patch, through the dry stane dyke and into the fields beyond. As we went, I turned my eyes briefly to the patch of earth where I had buried Trouble, three weeks earlier. He had been an old cat and ill for a long, harrowing time, before he slipped away in his sleep – but tonight, I had seen him back in his prime, the way I wanted to remember him. "Thanks," I said, trying to swallow the lump that again rose to my throat. All around us, there was movement and sound, as nature spirits went about their nightly business. Before I met John, I had no idea the countryside was so crowded. "He wanted to come and say goodbye," John explained. "All I did, was help you to see him."

Nevertheless, I was grateful. If John could bring that kind of comfort, then maybe I needn't feel so apprehensive. Maybe there was a point to his visits, other than to scare the life out of me. We walked on into the field, nodding politely to a passing Dryad, who studiously ignored us. I had learned, or at least John had told me, that most nature spirits have a complete disregard for humans and want nothing to do with their machinations. They just wanted to be left alone to do what they do. There were still some who were well disposed towards men, but these were a dwindling number, as mankind seemed intent on destroying them and all they held dear. On the other hand, the number of them inimical to humans, of which there had always been some, were swelling at an alarming rate. However, it seemed that tonight, the third consecutive full-moon that John had come for me, our destination lay further afield. On the far side of the field, on the farmer's track, was an old, black Austin Seven – what, in my youth, had been known as a box car (and they had been practically museum pieces even then – I hasten to add). "Come on!" John said. "Get in! We're going to town!"

John pulled open the driver's door and climbed in. The car was so small that he couldn't find an easy way to position his staff and finally had to place it diagonally with one end on the back seat and the other poking through his side window. I watched him struggle, using the time to try and think through this new development. We had never ventured much farther than about half a mile from my cottage before and all the time had been in the country. Surely a town would mean human spirits and I just didn't know if I could handle those, in any kind of numbers. True, we had encountered one such ghost – a cleric who had been murdered centuries ago on the banks of the Devon – but he had dwelt so long among the nature spirits that he had taken on their lack of interest in human affairs – and all but ignored us. I marvelled at how blasé I was becoming about these strange entities that I had encountered only a couple of months previously – and that had scared me rigid at the time. Maybe I placed my faith in John's protection and matter of fact approach. He had told me that my senses would become more acute as time went by and that soon, I would not need his presence to be aware of what was all around me. So far, not a lot had changed. I did catch glimpses, from time to time, at the edges of vision and heard indefinable, distant whispers – but nothing even remotely approaching the absolute clarity I experienced, with John as my guide.

In for a penny, in for a pound. Maybe a jolly jaunt in a rattly old ghost car, would be just the thing for a night's entertainment. After all, what did I have to fear? I started to walk round to the passenger's door, feeling quite at ease with myself and the cuddly world of the supernatural. In an instant, my smug complacency was blasted into oblivion. Something was near. I couldn't see it and I couldn't hear it – but I could feel it and smell it. It was real, it was evil and it was watching me. I froze, unable to move, even if my life depended on it –

and believe me, it felt like it did. It's hard to describe how it feels to be really, really mortally scared. Physically, everything seemed to have drained from my body and out through the soles of my feet. Lungs, heart, muscle and bone – all had gone and been replaced by solid ice. I couldn't breathe. I couldn't move, but strangely, my brain had gone into overdrive. Recriminations tumbled over themselves, in a race to gain my attention. Given the situation, all of them made perfect sense, even although they did nothing to change my predicament. Overriding them all, came the cold, clear realization that only my ignorance had made me feel secure. Just because, in my brief experience of this moonlit world, I had hitherto never met an actual threat, didn't mean they didn't exist. The proof was out there in the shadows, watching me and loathing what it was seeing. I have never felt such hatred. Then, as quick as it came, it was gone. I hadn't done anything to make it leave. God knows, I wouldn't have known where to start. One second it was there, the next it was gone and I was scrabbling at the door handle. Somehow, I got the door opened and collapsed into the passenger seat. As a cold sweat engulfed me, the car lurched into motion and John belatedly remembered to switch on the headlights.

My insides were still in turmoil as we reached the main road and made a left turn towards Dollar – although I had recovered enough to decide that I didn't want to play anymore. Just as I was about to make this sentiment known, John broke the silence. "It was a Hobgoblin," he told me. "They're nasty, but nowhere near as powerful as they like to make out. Most of what you felt, was just projection." It was hard to decide whether his conversational tone calmed me or irritated me. It was a close run thing. Anyway, he hadn't quite finished. "It's a bit worrying that they've found your home already – but maybe it was just coincidence." This did not make me feel any easier.

Once on the main road, we began to encounter traffic – a surprising amount of it. There were various types of horse-drawn vehicles and motor cars, that made John's Austin Seven look the height of modernity. None of these were moving very quickly. If John had waited in line, it would have taken us forever to get anywhere – but he didn't. He accelerated and drove straight on through them. "Don't worry," John told me. "It does them no harm. Most of them won't even be aware that we have passed through them and their vehicles." That wasn't my main concern. The cars, carts and coaches all looked solid to me – so much so, that I had frantically braced myself when we ploughed into the first few. I only hoped that John could tell the difference between a ghost vehicle and an actual solid road user.

In Dollar, we saw the first pedestrians – and there were a lot of them. They crowded the pavements. Some seemed to simply dawdle along whilst others looked purposeful in their stride. Such a variety of garb is hard to enumerate. I set myself to try and identify the when, in which these spectres had walked the streets in their flesh and blood bodies. Three walking together in a group defeated me. John noticed my attention on them and simply said, "Picts." There were Edwardians and Victorians. There were poorly dressed Peasants, Medieval Ladies and Warriors and plaid-clad, possible Jacobites. Most followed the route of present-day pavements but some just seemed to walk into walls and disappear. I was in awe-stricken wonderment. Soon though, we were through the village and back into the countryside. There were still a sprinkling of walking wraiths but not in the same volume as their urban compatriots.

Our route lay on the road that runs along the foot of the Ochil Hills. We passed through all the Hillfoot villages – Tillicoultry, Alva and Menstrie. At each one, the scene was broadly similar to what I had seen in Dollar. There were, obviously, more modern looking pedestrians and vehicles – so much so that I wasn't sure whether they were spectres or actual flesh and blood. For instance, just as we entered Tillicoultry, a modern fire-engine sped past, going in the opposite direction to us. Its blue lights were flashing and its siren blaring. "Is that real?" I asked my companion. "Yes," he replied, "It's a real ghost fire-engine." As we progressed, it became increasingly obvious that our destination was likely to be the ancient town of Stirling. I couldn't imagine the sheer volume of wraiths we were liable to encounter there – given its long ages of historical prominence.

At long last, I gathered myself sufficiently to ask the question that had been troubling me since first John had entered my life. "Why are you showing me all this?" I asked. "Why did you choose me?" John glanced sideways at me. "Ask yourself first," he said, "Why you have chosen to come with me and see the things that I have to show. You could have refused" I didn't have an immediate answer. After some thought, I finally replied. "Curiosity – I suppose." "Come, come," John said, "At least be honest with yourself, if not with me. Is it not, that you have reached a point in your life, where you hope for proof, that death is not the end of existence – that there is more to creation than the humdrum world of fleshly beings? Does it not comfort you to see evidence of otherworldly presences – that consciousness may indeed survive bodily death? You see – I know about your cancer."

Despite all the supernatural marvels that John had shown to me, this last revelation almost floored me. I was indeed suffering from terminal cancer – a fact I had not shared with anyone. I had no-one really to share it with. How did my mysterious guide know? It probably should not have been such a shock to me. John was obviously not of this World – at least, not entirely. Who knows what esoteric means he had access to – what knowledge he could be party to? My initial question seemed to have launched John into professorial mode. "There are three kinds of human essences that may remain in this World after death," he told me. "The vast majority – like all we have seen so far tonight – are mere projections. They have no awareness. They do not see, think or feel anything whatsoever. Like a moving picture at the cinema, they are merely an image of people who once existed, re-enacting episodes from their earthly lives."

John paused for a moment and then went on, "There are however, sentient human spirits. These can interact with each other – and with the living. For the most part, these entities are benevolent enough and do no harm. Their numbers are few. Fewer still are the third kind. These are the malevolent dead. These human ghosts are capable of small mischiefs – the kind of thing that is often attributed to, what you call, poltergeist activity. But some are much, much more dangerous. They are inherently evil and are avid to visit their wickedness on the living. Consider this and consider also, that some Nature Spirits can be corrupted and grow powerful in their hatred of mankind. Then you will realise that the Shadow-World is a profound, constant and ever evolving threat to humanity. There is a precarious balance – and it's my role to make sure it does not tip too far." I had forgotten my original question, which John seemed to have neatly sidestepped – but I had another. "Are you a ghost then?" I asked. "No my friend," John answered with a laugh in his voice. "I'm something different."

By this time, we had passed through Menstrie and were approaching the outskirts of Stirling. The wraiths were already very numerous here. There seemed to be a preponderance of phantoms dressed in martial attire. They wore a variety of chain mail, leather armour, steel breastplates, helmets and carried spears axes and swords. I was fascinated. John gestured to our left with one hand. "Over there," he said. "Is where I lived before I was chosen. I was an Augustinian of Cambuskenneth Abbey. I remember watching the battle at Stirling Bridge. With our location, we saw it all clearly. It was brutal and bloody. Years later, I had several conversations with The Wallace himself. He lodged with us for a while, hiding from the English and traitorous Scots. I found the man erudite and courteous – not at all like he was later portrayed by his enemies. More years later, I was in the presence of King Robert Bruce himself. He held court at our Abbey, on the evening following his victory at the Bannock Burn. I was too humble to warrant any of his attention amongst such exalted company. Nevertheless, I saw him in the flesh. And I have since seen many Kings, Queens and other notables. So you see, my friend, I am very, very old."

I didn't know what to make of this information. It had been obvious that there was an eldritch facet to John's nature. He couldn't have shown me the things he had shown me otherwise. Still, I felt a shiver down my spine at what he had just told me. He seemed to be flesh and blood, though I couldn't be entirely sure of that. How could he be so old and still have a body? Once again, I didn't know if I wanted to be where I was. I had expected us to drive into the centre of Stirling – but that wasn't our destination. At the Causewayhead Roundabout, we turned right to go uphill. "You have nothing to fear from me," he said, possibly sensing my mounting apprehension. "I'm a Guardian. Only the wicked should dread my coming. There is one such, lurking amongst the trees of the Abbey Craig. I can no longer ignore his malevolent presence – so I go now, to deal with him and I have brought you along to witness it."

This did not fill me with enthusiasm. I should have demurred – but John had a forceful personality – and so, I meekly acquiesced. The Abbey Craig was a craggy hill, rising from the carseland and situated between Stirling and the Ochil Hills. It was on this hill that Wallace's men had awaited the English army, crossing the bridge over the River Forth, prior to the battle John had spoken of. The tower of The Wallace Monument now stood on the summit, in commemoration of this. There were many warlike shades milling around, when we stopped in the carpark and exited the car. There were others about also but the majority of phantoms seemed martial in nature. No doubt, waiting for battle would generate a deal of psychic energy. "Ignore these ones," John told me. "They are unimportant to our purposes right now. The one we are seeking, is uphill. I can feel him."

It seemed that John was not the only one who felt a presence. The spectres that surrounded us were showing signs of fear. From what John had said earlier, I presumed that these were merely the projections that he'd spoken of. How could they experience any emotion? Nevertheless, there was terror on their faces and they crowded to get down off the hill – away from whatever stalked the trees further up. John looked at me. "Yes, this is a bad one," he said. "It's time to finish him." I began to feel afraid myself. If this entity was evil enough to scare apparently mindless shades, what could he do to me? John took his staff and began to stride purposefully up the single track road that led to the summit. The hillside was thickly wooded and looked threatening in the silvery light of the moon. The rain had stopped but the wind was still gusting fitfully. It shook the trees and I detected an ominous whisper in the rustling of the leaves. Was it just my imagination?

John was getting away from me. I feared to go on – but I feared being left alone even more. I hurried to catch up with him. We were alone now and it felt uncanny and uncomfortable, not to be in the midst of crowding spirits. There was no sound, other than the whispering of the trees. This was unnerving. In a wooded area like this, there should have been singing dryads or the sounds of other nature spirits. There was nothing. "Stay close," John told me. "This is no preening Hobgoblin. This one can really harm you." "How reassuring", I thought. For long minutes we walked uphill. John looked relaxed but I was growing more and more afraid. I could sense the presence now. Its proximity was palpable. Every nerve in my body was telling me to flee. My legs grew heavier and I had to fight to drag them forward. My heart was pounding, fit to burst and fear filled my chest and stomach like a solid, cannonball of sheer irresistible dread.

Panic hovered close. I could physically feel waves of evil washing downhill and flowing over us. The end of my tether was close indeed. John suddenly stopped and I walked into his back. I couldn't speak for fear, that only inane gibbering would issue forth from my mouth. "He's here," John said – and I stopped breathing. A darkness was rushing down the hill towards us. It was coming very fast. I couldn't see an entity but I knew it was there. As it got closer, I could discern a more solid darkness in the heart of the black wave that hastened to engulf us. Suddenly, John seemed to grow in stature. Physically, I later realised, he hadn't changed at all, but his presence swelled, and I was no longer afraid.

The onrushing dark slithered to a halt just feet from us. At its core, the central nub seemed to be stripped of its murky mystery. It was revealed as a grey male figure. The spectre's face was hideous and made more so by the rictus of shock and terror that contorted it. Obviously, no-one had told him about John. I got the impression that the horror had thought he was charging down two foolhardy and vulnerable, puny humans. There was one puny human, but John was something else. My companion pointed the head of his staff towards the entity. He said some words that meant nothing to me and with a blinding white light, the apparition disintegrated. It was gone – along with the darkness which had enfolded it.

I was still a bit weak at the knees, as we turned around and walked back to the car. Once again, the throngs of everyday ghosts were all around us. I found it intriguing that these apparently empty images could be subject to fear. There was a lot I didn't understand. We got back into the Austin Seven and John set it in motion. As he drove, he spoke. "You asked me earlier, why I was showing you a glimpse into the supernatural. Consider this. You were once a soldier. You have never married. You have no close living relatives. You are all alone and you are dying. All of these factors make you a suitable candidate. You have other qualities also. That is why you have been chosen, just like I was seven centuries ago. If you accept, you will replace me when I go to my peace."

I was completely blindsided by John's words. So I said nothing. "Don't worry," he went on. "I am not asking you to make a decision right now. When I leave you tonight, you will not see me again for a while. I will give you time to consider your choice and to let the senses I've awakened in you develop on their own for a little. On the third full moon from tonight, I will return. When I do so, you must answer my question – yay or nay. If nay, then I will leave you alone and you can live out the remainder of your life – and then die. If yay, you will be imbued with great power and endowed with a fantastically long lifespan. I will be with you for the first few years – to teach and to guide. But be warned, not all adversaries can be so easily dispatched as tonight's. You will be called upon to combat evil ghosts, rogue spirits and even the occasional demon. You will see many wonders but you will ultimately be alone – so think long before arriving at your decision."

John took me home. As he dropped me off, he left me with the words, "You may be troubled by the hobgoblin we encountered earlier. Do not be afraid. You are strong enough to withstand him." With that, he left me and I went indoors for a much needed brandy. All of this happened three months ago. In the ensuing time, my physical health has deteriorated markedly. Tonight, I await John's return. I think my answer will be yay.

The Seven Chambers.

Come gather to me people. Come, list to my tale of things long tossed on the dark seas of time. I am Mallon son of Bran – Loremaster and Bard. I will tell you of a once powerful people fallen on bad times – of brother turning against brother – of love and hate – bravery and cowardice – a Sword of Power – a wizard and much else. Draw close, for I know much and you may learn. But, if you seek not knowledge, come anyway – to pass the weary hours, while the fire burns high and the night is dark. What better way to do so, than in tales of love and war – comedy and tragedy? Come near. Be still. Attend my story and if it pleases you – you will reward me. If not, then I'll move on and nothing lost, but your time and my efforts. But enough. If all are ready, I'll begin.

Long, long ago, when men were heroes and the world a better place, there lived a tribe who called themselves The Children of Mannan. They dwelt in lands, gifted to them, at the beginning of time, by their Father, the Sea-God Mannan. These were rich lands, fertile, supporting good crops and many cattle. But, they were also perilous – for enemies surrounded them and envious eyes were cast oft in their direction. Many were the raids mounted in search of plunder – but the Children of Mannan were strong and vigorous, like their great Forefather and all the raiders got for their share, was the sword, axe and lance. So it was, that enemies ceased their fruitless efforts and the Children of Mannan were left alone, to grow and prosper.

Years passed. Generations came and went. Slowly, the sea withdrew from the land of Mannan, until it stood several days journey off, with only the great river to the west, giving memory of it ever having been there. With the water's retreat, the influence of Mannan waned in the land and, if people thought of him at all, it was as some far-off legend or children's tale. On a hill, outside Caermannan – the chief village – was a single standing stone with a massive boulder placed on top. This had been raised by the Sea-God himself – and around it, festivals still took place, councils were held and kings enthroned – but this had become tradition and not true memory. The Children of Mannan continued to be strong and prosperous. Their lands were well governed and their lives ordered – but now they imagined that all this had been achieved by their own efforts – as indeed, much of it had. Forgetting their inspiration, they trusted only in what could be seen with their own eyes and held by their own hands. Thus, when bad times came, their spiritual strength was diminished and a sickness spread in their souls – setting generations of prosperity at nought.

The Children of Mannan were ruled by Kings. In these days of vast Kingdoms and large cities, you may think that title too grand. You may think "Chieftain" or "Prince" would suffice, but what you think matters not, for there were Kings in Mannan and the Crown passed from Father to Son. Now, the King needs must be wise and strong – not only to repel invaders but to keep his own people in order, as they were a mettlesome race. Though their own borders were no longer threatened, the Men of Mannan oft times rode on raids into the surrounding lands. This they did not for plunder or riches, but in search of adventure, battle and glory. They were, after all, a warrior people at heart. Throughout the golden age of Mannan, the Kings had never failed. It is true, that not all had been notably wise but these had been sufficiently strong to discourage anyone from seeking to take advantage. The less strong, had always been wise enough not to let it show. So, all in all, things worked fairly well and seemed like to do so for ever. Now, everyone knows, although nobody believes, that nothing lasts forever and what can go wrong, will go wrong. So it came to pass, as sure as night follows day (although that is not as sure as most people think) – but I digress. Anyway – it came to pass, as most people think, night follows day, that along came a King who was neither strong nor wise.

Kin Endor was no more foolish than most men and like most men he had virtues and vices. Time dims all things, so, even I, Loremaster that I am, cannot tell you what his virtues were – but of his vices, I can speak. He was lazy, frivolous, petulant, a glutton and a drunkard. During his reign, the government of Mannan went unattended, unless by those with sufficient self-interest to manipulate the King to their own advantage. So it was, that the land fell into chaos and order collapsed. The strong took from the weak and the weak went without – or perished. This did not happen overnight, but took almost twenty years to reach the state of which now I will tell. Twenty years may seem a long time, but in a history of centuries, it is a mere twinkling. Had the Children of Mannan remembered their roots and not thought only of worldly things, a dozen weak kings would not have destroyed them. As it was, one very nearly did.

Now, Endor's greatest sin was that he left no sons. Whether this was through lack of wisdom or strength cannot be said, but when he died, any final vestige of order died with him. It was every man for himself and against all others. Murder and robbery abounded. Travellers held to the left side of highways, keeping their sword hands ever towards the stranger. Commerce ceased. Villages and hamlets cut themselves off from others, caring only for their own defence. The land lay open to raiders and invasion. The Painted People, who surrounded the land of Mannan, grew ever bolder and their depredations ever more grievous. At last, the leaders of the Painted People came to realise that they need no longer look towards Mannan with envy, or be satisfied with what could be plundered in hurried raids. They could have it all. So it was, that they gathered together a vast host and swarmed into Mannan. The land fell before them and its once proud people were slain and enslaved. Let it be known, mind you, that many of the defenders sold their lives dearly and died warriors' deaths – but lacking support and brotherhood, their efforts were futile. In a very short time, most of Mannan was in the hands of the invaders. Only the capital, Caermannan and the lands surrounding it in the North, remained unassailed. It is to here, that we must now turn our eyes.

In the village of Caermannan lived the nephews of the late King, Endor – the twin brothers, Gilmar and Eldane. Had things gone right, one of these would now be ruling the troubled land and perchance things would have gone differently. This, however, was not the case and no authority remained, capable of enthroning a king – no matter how rightful, at the time of their Uncle's death. The brothers themselves, had been but children then, orphaned and cared for by Morgan, the village wise-woman. Now they were grown to full manhood – too late it would seem. Gilmar, the elder of the two by some minutes, often boasted, in his cups, that he would ride to Strivling and there recover Mannan's Great Sword. Thus to regain the realm – but this, he never did – for the peril was great. I will tell you of this sword and its keeper soon – but first you must know something of the brothers.

Twins they were, as I have told you – but twins more unlike, you'll never meet. Both were tall and well made – but there the likeness stood and no further. Gilmar was fair and blue-eyed, whilst Eldane was dark. Yet, on the inside, the darkness was Gilmar's. He was brave, handsome, a skilled warrior and horseman – but he was cruel, arrogant and selfish. Men feared Gilmar, as did women – but he was not loved, save by his cronies and bully-boys – men of like nature and lesser imitations of himself. It would be good to tell you that Eldane, in contrast, was loved by all. It would be good but untrue. Yes he was loved by some – mostly small children, not of an age to know any better and by Morgan, his Foster Mother – and of course, by Gwyn, the fairest of all the Daughters of Mannan. Some, among the women, were kind to him and valued his gentle nature but the men despised him. You see, Eldane was a coward –

and among a warrior people, there can be no greater sin. Whereas, Gilmar was treated with respect – albeit inspired by fear – Eldane received only contempt. Had he been sickly or infirm, then Eldane might have been forgiven, but he was neither of these. In fact, at sport and swordplay, he could match with the best in tournament and practice – but he would never ride to battle. He feared pain, he feared death, but most of all, he feared to kill. Yet despite this, he won the love of Gwyn and they were happy. People shook their heads and wondered at such beauty being thrown away on one so unworthy – but Gwyn cared not. She loved Eldane and he her. Together, they lived with Morgan and ignored, whenever they could, the jibes and mockeries of their neighbours.

Then came the news of invasion and people, in their fear, looked for a leader. Already, as I have told you, the painted hordes had swept through most of Mannan, so full scale defence was too late – but perhaps their village could yet be saved – and anyway, there was no place else to go. Tyr-Mannan was the word on everyone's lips. Surely, this was the time of prophecy and dread. Suddenly, people began to believe the children's tales and legends. They believed that, when Mannan had departed long ages ago, for his realms beneath the sea, he had left his sword, Tyr-Mannan, in the keeping of Velyn. Only the rightful King could reclaim the sword in time of dire need and use it to save his people. Velyn, the Wizard, so it is said, dwelt less than half a day's ride away, on the great rock of Strivling. It is there that the people, with one voice begged Gilmar to go – for, of course, he was the leader they had chosen.

Gilmar scoffed at their weakness and credulity – though he did accept the leadership. "Are you children, to believe such nonsense?" he ridiculed. "There is no magic sword and none is required. Are we not warriors? Have you all turned to old women or to snivelling cowards, like he with whom I shared a womb but not my spirit. What are a few painted savages? I, Gilmar, will lead you to victory. So forget all such foolishness and make ready for battle.

For a short time, the people were cheered and those who remembered Gilmar's earlier belief in the sword – and his drunken boasts of recovering it – chose to forget them as unsafe or inconvenient. In truth, however, Gilmar did believe in the sword and was troubled. He knew that winning Tyr-Mannan was not a simple matter of lineage or claim to the crown. Whoever entered on that quest, would be severely tested. Failure would bring destruction and torment – terrible and eternal. There could only be one – and he must be worthy. In his heart, for all his arrogance, Gilmar doubted himself. So he chose destruction for his people and a warrior's death, rather than face the consequences of failure.

Soon it mattered not what Gilmar believed, for the Painted People had come and all hope was gone. The warriors of Mannan were strong brave and skilled – none more so – but their numbers, compared to the host that surrounded them, were as the leaves on one tree to that of the leaves in a vast forest. Yet, still did the respect and fear, learned through the long ages, hold back the Painted People. They sat in the hills around the village, gathering their courage yet awhile, before attacking.

The first day passed thus and was followed by a night of dread – wherein the sky glowed blood-red with the myriad fires of the Painted People and their savage chanting filled the air, to the ceaseless throbbing of countless drums. No-one in the village slept that night. Each prepared to meet their fate, in whichever way best suited his or her nature. Some made love. Some buried their treasures. Some just waited and some even prayed. The warriors? Well, for the most part, they got drunk and boasted, as warriors are wont to do. All such preparation and apprehension proved unnecessary – at least for the time being, for on the morrow, no attack came. Day dawned and noon came – but still nothing happened. So it was that Gilmar summoned the villagers to the speakers' mound – that he might address them.

"Children of Mannan," he said. "It is not honourable for warriors, such as we, to sit like cattle awaiting the knife. I, for one, will have none of it."

At this, a lusty cheer interrupted him and delayed his oration for some minutes. It must be said, curiously enough, that the women, children and elders, who had not spent the night drinking, were less enthusiastic in their approbation. Nevertheless, Gilmar eventually continued.

"To-night, under the cloak of darkness, I will lead forth the men of Caermannan to take up position on the Sea God's Hill. There, around Great Mannan's Stone, we will keep our vigil. Come the dawn, all will see how heroes die.

Again the cheers and again the same people cheering. As the acclamation died down, a lone voice rang out and all others fell silent. It was Eldane who spoke – and the silence came not from respect but from astonishment at his daring to speak at all.

"Surely this is folly," he said, somewhat abashed at the sudden quiet but nonetheless continuing, "We have already wasted too much time. Ditches should be dug and the village barricaded….."

It is likely that Eldane had more to say and perhaps there was wisdom in his words – but these were drowned by the curses and howling of those who had cheered his brother – and little wonder. For this was not the way for warriors to fight. Warriors died gloriously, facing overwhelming odds – not hiding behind barricades. That was craven's death – a merchant's death – a cow's death. None would sing songs of such a death.

As I look around your faces, I see many things. So I will pause in my story, for just a moment. Some of you approve of Gilmar's plan and may even hope that unlooked for salvation will arrive for the Children of Mannan. Perhaps that means you are just like they. Whether that reflects credit, I will leave to your own consideration. Others among you will be thinking, that they were not a particularly worthwhile race and mayhap deserved their coming extinction. You too are entitled to your thoughts. Perhaps there are yet others listening, who realise I have only described the people in broad terms. You will know that among any people, there would be good and bad, worthy and unworthy, wise and foolish. Even Gilmar was not all bad nor Eldane all craven. So you may think – and you might be right or wrong. Then again – maybe you would be neither. The answers to these questions may become clearer as my story unfolds – but one thing I can say, what happened next was bad – very bad indeed.

As the jeers of the warriors died down, Gilmar strode from the mound, his face twisted in fury. The people parted in fear before him, until he came to where Eldane and Gwyn stood together.

"You, my false brother, will stay behind with the women and children," he roared in a voice distorted with rage and hate. "Whilst the men go to do men's work. But she," he turned to Gwyn, "All know she is wasted on you. So now she is mine and will know what a man can do. With that, he seized Gwyn and dragged her towards the mound – for this had long been in his heart. Then did a change come on Eldane. For a cold fury filled him and his hand fell to the dagger at his belt. Who knows what might then have fallen out, had not Eldane been dispatched into darkness by a blow from a club wielded by one of Gilmar's toadies. Gwyn struggled and cried for help but to no avail. For the people of Caermannan turned from her and – to their everlasting shame, left her to her fate. Not so, Gilmar's cronies, for they were inflamed and beyond compassion and decency. So it was that, despite, or mayhap because of her struggles, Gwyn was used violently and shamefully by Gilmar – and afterwards by those despicable others who were his friends.

Let us now draw a veil over the remainder of that terrible day. You may think that a more terrible one promised to follow – and to some degree you would be right – but the Painted People were enemies, from whom such behaviour might be expected – never from your own. Night fell and the warriors of Mannan departed. Some indeed, felt shame for not having intervened – but by now, it was too late. In the hut of Morgan, the wise woman, Eldane stirred. He had lain unconscious since that fearful blow – and as yet, knew nothing of what had happened. Slowly, painfully, he sat up.

"So, you are back with the living at last," Morgan said – her voice sounding less than kind. "You have slumbered over long, my adopted son – even before this day. But now, it is time to be up and doing."

Eldane turned towards the voice, with eyes that could not both look in the same direction. Wherever his wits were, they had not yet returned to his head. For some time he sat thus, seeking to make out shapes in the hut's dim interior. Suddenly, vision and memory returned as one and Eldane knew fear.

"Where is Gwyn?" he rapped out, his tongue feeling too big for his mouth.

Morgan sat beside Eldane's pallet and despite her tone, her expression, though grave, was not unkind. Wordless, she stepped aside. Gwyn lay on another pallet, pale and unmoving, a sheepskin drawn up to her chin. Eldane's heart froze. He leapt from bed, stumbling in his dizziness, and knelt beside her. Tears sprang to his eyes and tumbled down his cheeks, as he tenderly pushed back the hair from Gwyn's bruised but ashen face.

"Is she dead?" he asked.

"No, but she has been ill used and has taken many hurts," came the reply. "She still hangs on, but I cannot say for how long."

After a moment, Eldane spoke again.

"Tell me all," he said.

Morgan did, sparing no detail and Eldane listened, growing colder with every word. At length he arose and walked shakily to where his sword hung on the wall. Taking it down, he turned towards the door.

"Where are you going?" Morgan asked.

"I go to see my brother," came the grim reply.

"Fool! Will killing him bring Gwyn back to life?"

"No – but I and the world will feel better for it."

"And what of the Children of Mannan? Will you also leave them to their fate – leaderless and with no hope?"

"I care not for the Children of Mannan," he spat out. "They are not worthy to survive and well merit their fate.

Morgan, in her turn, grew angry. "And I suppose you are worthy, oh righteous one," she exploded. "You, who have done nothing all your life. You , who could have stayed Gilmar's hand years ago. You, who could have united the people. You, who should be King. Judge not others, Eldane, before you judge yourself. Did you think the Painted People would be more gentle with your lady – or on any of the other women and girls? Go then, fool. Slay your brother and be slain. For you are beyond hope or reason."

Eldane stopped, stunned by Morgan's unexpected tirade. "What else can I do?" he asked. "It is too late to save Gwyn." His fury fled and was replaced by sorrow. He crossed again to Gwyn's bed and looked upon her.

"Stir yourself, man," came Morgan's voice. "All is not yet lost but will be if you stand there weeping like some lovesick maiden."

Eldane turned to Morgan. "There is nothing I can do," he said. "Is there?"

Morgan uttered a fearful oath, which I cannot here repeat.

"Of course there is, you great dolt," she continued. "Ride for Strivling! Bring back the Sword! Tyr-Mannan gives life, as well as taking it away! It can restore Gwyn. Nothing else will."

"But," said Eldane and got no further. "Ride for Strivling," Morgan interrupted. "Epona is outside, waiting, saddled for you. Ride to Strivling. Seek out the She-Wolf. She will lead you to Velyn. Bring back the Sword. It is the only way to save Gwyn. Ride now and you can be back by morning. Delay – and all is lost. In Mannan's name, go, go, GO!!"

She glared at Eldane, who still stood unmoving. Then a resolve seemed to settle on him. "Yes, I will go," he said. "For Gwyn, I would dare anything."

Pausing only to stoop and kiss Gwyn's forehead, he turned and strode from the hut.

"I'll be back before morning," He called over his shoulder, and was gone.

Morgan listened to the hoofbeats fading into the night, offered up a silent prayer and turned to tend Gwyn, as best she could.

Meanwhile, Eldane set his horse's head towards Strivling and urged her forward. Epona was a dappled grey mare – but in the moonlight, she shone like silver. To look upon, she was ungainly and clumsy – but looks can deceive. For, when Epona stretched her long legs and flew across the ground, no other steed, in all the lands, could hope to match her. A grim determination had come upon Eldane and this was mirrored on his face. Before long, they came to where the Painted People waited – as of course they must do, for these were all around. Providence led them on a path less well guarded than most – although still held in sufficient numbers. But, a fear fell on the Painted People at their coming and they withdrew – to speak, in hushed tones, of the grey ghost with eyes of fire, who galloped his phantom, shining steed through the long night.

On and on went horse and rider, never slackening pace, through field and forest, bog and stream. On they thundered, while the night passed and the moon climbed ever higher. Eldane knew not the hour and lost all sense of time – even though it was the enemy and must be outstripped. They, at last reached the edge of the flat carselands and paused momentarily in their headlong flight. There before them, still at some distance, rose the great rock of Strivling – silhouetted in the moonlight. Then, they were off again, shooting across the plain like an arrow, from some giant bow.

Presently Eldane drew rein, for they had come to the foot of the rock and he knew not which way to proceed. Strivling stood high, with many crags and precipices. Legend told, that there were several paths, leading up and through the rock, but only one led to the dwelling place of Velyn. The others were perilous to the unwary and like to bring such to disaster. In any case, Eldane could not spare precious time, exploring ways, which might come to a dead end – or worse. He remembered Morgan's words. Leaning forward, Eldane whispered into the horse's ear.

"Seek out and take me to the She-Wolf, good Epona, if you will. For time runs on and my need is great."

Let it be known, before any mock, that the Children of Mannan were kindred to the horse, and that these creatures were almost human. In fact, some would say more than human – for they had none of the meanness of spirit, common amongst men. Epona, who was not the least of her race, whinnied once in answer, before raising her head and sniffing the night air. Satisfied, she turned and trotted along the edge of the rock.

Before long, Eldane realised that they were not alone. All around them, grey shapes weaved silently, in and out of the darkness – keeping pace with their progress. At first, the shapes stayed at the very edges of vision – but seemed to become bolder as they moved along. Soon, there was no doubt. They were surrounded by wolves, who escorted – or perhaps stalked them, through the night. Eldane drew courage from Epona, who seemed not at all put out by the closeness of so many of her natural enemies. At times, Eldane fancied that he heard whisperings on the night wind – as though the wolves called to him to come join them and run with the pack. He dismissed this as merely the wind playing tricks, as it blew through the gullies and crannies. But it grew more insistent and seemed to say,

"Come with us, young warrior."

"Come run with us."

"Throw off your skin."

"Come hunt with us."

"Do not resist."

"Come feast with us."

"Do not resist."

"For soon you must come run with us."

The voices seemed to chant in rhythm to the panting of the grey beasts that flanked them. It never seemed to grow louder, only more intense. Eldane, although somewhat unnerved, could not be certain whether he truly heard them or if his fancy played him tricks. Then, abruptly, the voices ceased. Epona slowed to a stop and their escort slunk off into the darkness. Eldane's eyes were drawn upwards, in the direction of the rock – and for a moment, his heart misgave him. There, on a crag, stood the She-Wolf. Black as the night she was and huge, twice the size of her common brethren. Her massive shoulders hunched, as she regarded them, head down, her lips drawn back revealing a fearsome array of gleaming fangs. But worst of all were her eyes, for they glowed blood-red in the darkness. For a moment in time, they stood frozen thus and Eldane wondered what to do next. He would have spoken but his mouth had gone dry and he dared not trust it. Nevertheless, the creature seemed to divine his purpose – for in one sinuous movement, it leaped from the crag, about two men's height, and landed before them. Epona never gave a flinch, although the same cannot be said of her rider. The great beast turned and loped into the night, bidding them follow in a voice that horse and man heard only in their heads, but both understood.

Presently, they turned from the path they had been using into another and thus began their ascent of Strivling. The She-Wolf never once looked back but continued on her way, seemingly careless whether horse and rider kept up, or not. Doubts began to assail Eldane as to his ability to complete this matter – though his determination to attempt it never wavered. Already, he had known much fear and the test had not yet even begun.

The path was broad and easy, to begin with, but soon it steepened and narrowed. At times, it was indeed perilous, with a sheer rock face rising on one side and an equally sheer drop awaiting on the other. Often, Eldane had to bend low over his mount's neck in order to avoid overhanging ledges or unexpected bushes which threatened to sweep him from the saddle. He never once thought of dismounting however, and that was just as well, for Epona was more sharp eyed and sure footed than any mere human and, after what seemed an age, she brought him safely to the summit and to Velyn. If Eldane had expected some noble sage, attired in priestly vestments, he was sorely disappointed. Instead, he found an old man, dressed in rags, with straggly beard and hair, crouching beside a huge blazing fire. The She-Wolf went to this tattered looking individual and stretched herself on the ground beside him, luxuriating in the warmth of the fire. He reached out a hand, absent mindedly and scratched behind one of her enormous ears. Eldane had been rehearsing his introduction over and over but suddenly felt a bit taken aback and tongue tied. Before he could pull himself together, the old man spoke.

"Well, Eldane of Mannan," he said in a querulous voice. "What brings you here, disturbing our peace in the night, like this? I suppose you've come to try for the Sword. Eh?"

Eldane nodded his head and was about to speak when the old man cut in again.

"Not a good time, if you ask me, but no-one ever does. Anyway – I'm Velyn, by the way and I'm the Keeper. Don't think you're the first either. Lots have tried and none have done it. Still want to try?"

Eldane nodded again and this time managed to blurt out a yes before Velyn continued.

"Well, get off your horse then. It's too narrow and dangerous for it in there.

Eldane dismounted and stood uncertainly. "What must I do?" he asked.

"There is no *"must do"*. You can ride away or fly in the air, for all I care. No-one ever comes to see me unless they're looking for something. If it's not the Sword, then it's a love potion or a magic charm or "tell me my future". It's never, "how are you today, Velyn" or "here's a nice present for you Velyn" or....."

This was not going at all the way Eldane expected and he began to grow impatient – and even more nervous. "Hold!" he said, interrupting Velyn's tirade. "My need is pressing, old man. My time runs short. Tell me what I must do to win the sword."

There was a sudden silence at his words and he all but regretted saying them. The old man glared at him – and worse – so did the fearsome She-Wolf at his side.

"Old man, is it? You lack respect, young Eldane," Velyn said, his voice menacing. "Very well – here is what you must do – or try to do. You will enter the rock through a door which I will open for you. There are seven chambers, cut in the heart of the rock. In each, you will face a test. If you succeed, you pass to the next chamber. If you fail, your fate will be very unpleasant. If you do what no other has ever managed – and pass through all seven, then you will be worthy of Tyr-Mannan – and we will speak again. Remember though, Eldane of Mannan, it is ordained that only one can succeed. Are you the one?"

Now, if you live your life basking in the admiration of others, you soon come to believe that you are indeed a fine fellow and worthy of that admiration – but not so Eldane. In the eyes of his people, he saw only contempt – and therefore imagined that these were mirrors, reflecting his true self. But in the eyes of Gwyn, he saw something else and maybe that would sustain him.

"I know not, Velyn, if I am worthy," he answered. "I only know, I have to try."

"Very well then," Velyn said. "Come with me."

They walked to a small mound that lay just at the edge of the campfire's light. Without any fuss or ceremony, Velyn passed a hand over the mound and an opening appeared, revealing stairs leading down into the rock's interior. Eldane was about to step forward, when the old man restrained him.

"Just a moment. I forgot something," he said, scuttling back in the direction of the fire and calling, "Wait here!" over his shoulders. Eldane licked his lips nervously and gazed into the darkness below. His insides felt like he had swallowed live eels, that wriggled in a most unpleasant manner. Had Velyn been a heartbeat or two longer in his return, then perhaps the quest would have been over before it had begun.

"Take this," Velyn said, thrusting a smooth heavy object into Eldane's hands.

Eldane drew his eyes from the opening in the ground and examined the object. It was a crystal skull, about the size of a man's and of exquisite workmanship.

"What is it?" he asked.

"Not what – who," came the reply. "His name is Buffmet, or some such – and he will be your guide. Listen to him well, for he will tell you no lies – though he may not tell all the truth."

With that, the old man bundled Eldane towards the stairs. "Go now and face your demons – and good luck," were the last words Eldane heard before the mound closed over him and he was in total darkness. Suddenly, there were so many questions that Eldane wanted to ask, including how Velyn had known his name, but now it was too late. Cautiously, with the crystal skull tucked under one arm and his other hand stretched out to the wall for balance and comfort, Eldane began his descent, feeling gingerly with his feet before taking each step.

Again, Eldane lost track of time and distance, as he went ever downwards. The stairs seemed endless. Then somehow, despite his caution, Eldane contrived to trip. Down he tumbled, letting go of the skull and taking several bruises in the process. It might have gone ill, but luck was with him – for he had not far to fall before fetching up on a floor or landing. He knew not which. Despite the bruises, no serious damage was done and presently Eldane rolled over onto his hands and knees, ready to stand up. As he did so, he became aware of a greenish glow, just a little way off, which grew stronger moment by moment. In wonder, he realised it was the skull, which was soon shining brightly enough to light the cavern in which he knelt. It seemed to Eldane, that he was in an entry hall, with roughhewn walls, about ten paces away in either direction. Behind him were the stairs and ahead, a doorway.

Without warning, the skull floated up from the floor and came to a stop, level with Eldane's face.

"That was a bit unnecessary," it said. "You only had to speak to waken me – not bounce me off every rock in Strivling."

Eldane never flinched. He was too surprised to do so.

"I'm sorry," he said. "I tripped."

"Well, try not to be so clumsy. You've given me quite a headache," said the skull.

"Sorry," Eldane mumbled.

"Anyway, to business," the skull said. "Do you know who I am?"

"Yes. The old man called you Buffmet and said you would be my guide."

"Baphomet – Baphomet," said the skull, sounding quite peevish.

"My name is Baphomet and after a thousand years, you'd think the old goat would get it right. My name is Baphomet and it means "The Father of Knowledge". I know all things – past, present and still to come. Go on. Ask me something. I'll allow you one question, just to prove it."

Eldane had drawn himself up into a sitting position. He considered for a moment.

"Do you know if I'll succeed in my quest?" he asked.

"Yes, I do," came the reply.

Eldane waited. Baphomet remained silent. At last, Eldane prompted him.

"Well?"

"Well what?"

"Will I succeed?"

"That is another question. I've already told you I know, which is what you asked – so don't be greedy. I don't normally do even one test question – so don't try to badger me into two."

Eldane framed a reply but thought better of it. Instead, shaking his head, he stood up. Baphomet floated to head height and began moving off towards the door.

"I'd advise you to draw your sword now, young man," he said. "For, I'm about to introduce you to Malgrath. It means slayer. I think you'll like him."

Feeling anything but happy, Eldane drew his sword and followed.

The door opened at their approach and they entered the first chamber. It was about twice the size of the entry hall and its walls glowed lurid red. In the far wall, Eldane could see the exit door and beside it a large alcove, part covered by a hide screen. He looked around, in growing dismay, at the bones and parts of bones which littered the chamber's floor. Obviously, he was not the first to come this way. Then the hide curtain was torn aside and a creature of nightmare stepped forth. It was man shaped, standing half again as tall as Eldane, with massive shoulders and huge, muscular limbs, covered with coarse, black hair. The rest of its body was covered, from tree-trunk neck to mid-thigh, by a tunic of mail but its head was bare – aye – and what a head, for Malgrath had the head of a serpent, huge, black and loathsome. His eyes shone yellow, and between them protruded a single curved horn. In his hands, he carried the most fearsome blade Eldane had ever set eyes on. This he hefted expertly and easily, making the air sing with its passage. For a moment, Eldane thought of retreat but sensed that the way behind him was barred. The only way out, was forward.

"This is Malgrath," Baphomet said, before retreating to safety, just below the ceiling. "I'm afraid you must fight him but don't be put off by appearances. He's much worse than he looks."

The time for fear was past, for the monster attacked. Eldane barely managed to avoid being swept away at the first onslaught. Somehow, he contrived to dodge and parry the blows that rained on him, though his sword arm was numbed at the shock of their force. Briefly, Eldane disengaged, before returning to the business of staying alive. He knew this could not go on much longer – and then he had no time to think of anything else, for the fight was on again.

Soon, Eldane could hardly hold his sword, as Malgrath redoubled his efforts. The end was very near. Death approached rapidly. Again, there was a moment of respite, as Malgrath drew off, to ready for the final onslaught. Then, a strange thing happened. Eldane ceased to care and with that ceased to think. He took his sword in a two-handed grip and waited. His mind was calm. No thoughts of victory or defeat – life or death, clouded his spirit. Malgrath attacked and battle was truly joined. Remember, that Eldane was a trained and skilled swordsman, though not, up to now, a warrior. Now he was changed. Whether it had always been, or whether the emotions of the last few hours had wrought it in him, I know not. All I know is, that Eldane had achieved that state, sought after by all who follow the way of the warrior. He was one with his sword. He was one with his enemy. He was one with the battle. Victory and defeat are overlapping parts of the same oneness. Victor and vanquished are not separate, but joined by the combat. It mattered not, which part you played.

So the fight went on and it was fearsome to behold, as they whirled in their grim dance of death. The sound of steel on steel echoed and re-echoed from the cavern's walls and sparks flew, as blade clashed on blade. Long they fought thus and so matched were they, that neither drew blood. But end it must and end it did. Malgrath overstretched himself and his guard was down. In Eldane's mind, the next blink of an eye, took place with dreamlike slowness. His sword rose in a back hand sweep and sliced cleanly through Malgrath's bull-like neck, sending the hideous serpent head spinning lazily through space, whilst fountains of dark, thick blood seemed to hang forever in the air.

The moment passed and time returned to normal. With a crash, Malgrath's headless body buckled at the knees and fell to the ground. Eldane would have done likewise, had he not his sword to lean on for support. He staggered to a spot, away from the lake of blood that threatened to cover the chamber's floor, and sat down heavily. Eldane began to tremble at the import of what had occurred and the realization that he still lived. It was as if someone else – and not he – who had taken part in the combat. For a moment, everything felt out of focus and unreal.

"Come on. No time to rest. The next chamber awaits." It was Baphomet.

Eldane regarded the floating head for a moment

"Does it get worse?" he asked.

"Well, that depends."

"Depends on what?"

"On whether or not you succeed, of course," said Baphomet. "By the way, I should have mentioned that his sword was poisoned – but I forgot in the heat of the moment. Still – no harm done."

With that, he floated towards the door. Wearily, Eldane got up and followed. Beyond the door was a short passage, leading to another entrance. Baphomet sank to the floor.

"I will rest here a while, though you must go on," he said.

"Aren't you coming with me?" asked Eldane, somewhat alarmed.

"No. I – ah – wouldn't want to put you off, or anything."

Eldane was not at all reassured by this.

"Can you tell me nothing?" he asked anxiously.

"Of course I can. Don't be so impatient. I was just coming to it. Firstly, you can put away your sword, for you won't be needing it. Secondly, the – ah – person you will meet in there, will speak only the truth. I can say no more. You must go on." Feeling little joy, Eldane nevertheless sheathed his sword and entered the second chamber.

Sweet music filled his ears and subtle perfumes floated on the air. In size, this chamber resembled the last – but there the similarity ceased. Everything spoke of beauty and ease. The walls were hung with soft, translucent fabrics, through which emanated a peaceful, rosy luminescence and the floor was strewn with sheepskins and costly rugs. A small fountain tinkled pleasantly – its waters sparkling in pastel hues, from cunningly positioned coloured lanterns. Despite himself, Eldane felt tension ebb away. Beyond the fountain, a handful of steps led to a raised area, concealed by curtains, through which shone a warm amber light. As Eldane watched, the curtains slowly drew asunder – and then he saw her. His breath caught for a moment, for she was beautiful. Gracefully, the woman rose from the couch on which she sat and stretched her hands towards him.

"Welcome Eldane," she said – and her voice was sweeter than the music. "My name is Elenor and I would comfort you. Come – sit awhile and rest from your struggles. Refreshed, you will make better speed in your quest. Come...."

Eldane saw wisdom in her words and found the prospect pleasing. "A little time will do no harm," he told himself. "I will not delay long."

He advanced towards her and she came to meet him at the foot of the steps. Taking both his hands in hers, Elenor led Eldane up to the couch and bade him sit.

"You will take a measure of wine, my lord?" she said smiling.

Eldane nodded, wordless and watched as she poured the wine from a pitcher into two goblets, which sat on a small table beside the couch. She wore a simple dress of fine, white cotton, which left one shoulder bare and, in truth, did little to conceal the shape, if not the substance, of what lay beneath. Yet, there was an innocence in her brown eyes and perfect features, which spoke of maidenly virtue, rather than temptress. Her hair was long and black as the night, contrasting with the white of her dress and enhancing both. Eldane felt at ease. Her company was pleasing and carried no threat, or at least, so he told himself.

For a time, they sipped wine and talked. Eldane could not have told you on what they conversed, only that the sweetness of her voice and maidenly laughter, enthralled him and made his troubles and worries seem far away. The music, soft light, perfumes and wine combined to lull his senses. Time ceased to matter.

Elenor poured more wine and Eldane raised no objection. As she handed him the goblet, their fingers brushed. She was sitting very close now and he could feel the warmth of her body and smell the heady fragrance of her perfume. Strange that he hadn't noticed before the knowing glint in her eye, nor realised how husky and teasing was her voice. Even the music seemed different – somehow more insistent, wilder. He felt himself stirring and tried to resist it, but could not remember why.

"I, I must be going," he said, trying to stand up. "There's something important I must do."

Elenor held him back.

"Do not go, Eldane," she said. "Put aside such foolish fancy. Stay with me and I will unlock passions in you, beyond your dreams. Be my lover and I will show you pleasures you did not know existed."

A flame was burning in Eldane and her words fanned it to a blaze – but still he wavered. This was not right. There was something important – something terribly important – but what? Elenor stood up. "Watch me and be convinced," she said. The music changed again and the rhythm of a drum insinuated itself into the melodies. Elenor stepped back and began to dance. At first, she swayed slowly in time with the drum and Eldane sat, captivated. Imperceptibly, the tempo quickened and so did the dance. A second drum joined in playing counterpoints and the melody swelled. Wilder and wilder grew the dance, louder and louder grew the music. Elenor writhed and whirled, swayed and stepped. The drums throbbed. The light glowed scarlet and the smell of lust hung in the air. Eldane's blood pounded in his ears and his fevered vision never left the object of his desire. The dress slipped from Elenor's shoulder and fell to the floor – but still she danced, never losing rhythm. She moved towards Eldane and he stood ready to receive her. Their eyes locked and it was as if nought else existed. Her face loomed close in Eldane's sight. And then, unbidden, a fleeting vision came to him. He saw another face, pale, bruised and near to death – a face he loved. The spell was broken. "No!" he cried, dashing the goblet, he still held, to the floor. Immediately, the music died. Then were his eyes opened – for the cloth hangings were cobwebs, the rugs, sack cloth and the fountain ran red with blood. The couch was an outcrop of rock and the perfume was the cloying stench of death. Yet, Elenor stood before him, but her eyes were changing. Their rich brown was turning to red and beginning to glow. She fell forward onto all fours and began to grow. Dark hair sprouted all over her body and her perfect features elongated into a snout. As Eldane watched, horrified, the transformation was complete – and there before him, stood the She-Wolf. She fixed him with a baleful look and, gathering herself, leapt high over his head and was gone.

For some time, Eldane stood there, unseeing and unhearing, in his shock, Until Baphomet finally roused him.

"Come on. Come on," said the skull. "Two down, five to go. Come on. Time to be moving."

Eldane looked at Baphomet and knew anger.

"You played me false," he snarled.

"Nonsense. How so?" came the reply.

"You told me that she would not lie but all this was false – a lie. You played me false."

"Really, young man – you must learn to listen," said Baphomet. " I said she would *SPEAK* only the truth and so she did. If you had lain with her, you would have become like her, a wolf. Then, you would have known passions undreamed of and pleasures unimagined. I'm sure you must have met some of your predecessors, her husbands, on your journey. Did they not call to you? They usually do. Anyway, time to be off. What is your name anyway? I can't go on calling you thingummy or young man, all the time."

"I thought you knew everything," Eldane said but Baphomet was not listening. Already, he was half way to the next door.

Again a short passageway and again another door opened at their approach. This time, both entered together. The third chamber had the same dimensions as the previous two but seemed smaller because it was so tightly packed. A single flaming torch, fixed high on the wall, served for illumination – but the chamber was not dim. The caverns contents reflected and indeed magnified the torchlight – so that the very air seemed to shine with a coruscating golden light, shot through with sparkling reds, greens and blues. Never before, or since, has such wealth been gathered together in one place. Everywhere Eldane looked, his eyes fell on gold and precious jewels. All manner of priceless artifacts abounded. Overflowing chests of gold coins, spilled their contents on the floor. Emeralds, sapphires and rubies lay in piles – some separate and some intermingled. There were golden, gem encrusted goblets, plates to match, bracelets, diadems, body adornments of all kinds – even armour – and all of shining gold.

Eldane was struck dumb. He could not imagine the existence of so much wealth in all the world – let alone here, in one room. Baphomet spoke, startling Eldane back to his senses.

"You have a choice to make here, young man," he said. "And if you'll pop your eyes back into their sockets and raise your chin from the floor, I'll explain it." Eldane composed his features and gave Baphomet his attention.

"You may not have noticed, but in the far wall, there is not one, but two doors."

Eldane looked and so that this was so.

"Now, if you choose to continue your quest, you must take nothing from here and leave by the left hand door. If not – all that is here is yours and you may depart in safety by the other door.

"There is no choice," said Eldane. "I must go on – but I'm curious. What is the trick?"

"How do you mean?"

" There is something you are not telling me. There always has been till now. Will the gold turn to sand or some such? Is it all an illusion?"

"No trick, young Eldane. The treasure is real. Beyond that door there are carts and oxen for transport. There are porters and an armed escort to take you wherever you want to go. The choice is yours. Continue your perilous quest, with no certainty of survival, or depart, to live out your years in ease and luxury. This is your last chance. If you choose the quest, you must complete it or perish. There will be no way out."

"Without Gwyn, there is no life, so what use is wealth?"

"Be not hasty. Wealth brings many things, apart from ease. It brings freedom. It brings power. Come, I will show you."

The skull led Eldane to a corner, wherein stood a large mirror of burnished gold.

"Stand before the mirror and tell me what you see."

Eldane did so. "I see myself," he said.

"You see yourself as you are now, Eldane," responded Baphomet. "And what is that? I will tell you. You see a man who is often unhappy and frustrated, because he does not think like others of his people and is powerless to do anything about it. You see a man who believes himself in love. Gwyn has been kind to you but do you love her or are you merely grateful. You believe that Gwyn loves you, but at times you wonder whether she respects you. Would she not prefer someone braver – a man of action – a warrior? At times, you believe yourself content – but is that true contentment, or ignorance of anything better? Watch – and I will show you what you could be."

The mirror darkened and seemed to shimmer. Then a picture formed and it was like gazing through a window – for Eldane could see and hear everything that passed.

"This could be you, one year hence," explained Baphomet. "If you choose wealth."

Eldane saw himself reclining at ease on a couch of sumptuous velvets. He was dressed in the finest of raiments and wore golden adornments, fit for an emperor. The couch seemed to sit in a magnificent pavilion, with furnishings both costly and exquisite. In his hand was a golden goblet, from which he drank rich, red wine. Dancing girls were before him and servitors hastened to do his every bidding. The mirror darkened and a new vision formed.

"I take you forward ten years," said Baphomet, "To when you have built your Capital and Palace."

The vision showed a great city of shining marble. Everywhere, was order and beauty. The people, not a race familiar to Eldane, looked well-fed and happy. Then he saw a palace that could have no peer anywhere. Its gilded towers and domes shone in the sunlight and windows of wonderous stained glass seemed to glow with an inner light. People strolled on the broad lawns and gardens, amidst dancing fountains and beautiful statuary. For a moment, the vision lingered and then they were in the throne room. Such opulence, such carvings, such craftmanship defied description. Eldane sat on the throne and his dress was even more magnificent than before. On his head was a circlet of gold. Around him were advisors, men at arms, musicians, dancers, tumblers and servants of all descriptions. He received petitioners and ambassadors, people of distinction – but all bowed low and deferred to Eldane. The vision faded and the mirror was once again only a mirror.

"Well," said Baphomet. "Make your choice,"

"Hold, Baphomet. I will not yet tell you of my decision – for – you see – I do not trust you."

Eldane raised a hand, before Baphomet could respond and went on. "You may not exactly lie to me, but you don't always speak all the truth. I know not if there is a purpose to this or if it be but your nature. Twice now, you have called me by my name, which you earlier implied you did not know. So – I desire that you re-awaken the mirror and show me one more thing."

Baphomet spluttered – if that is possible for a disembodied skull – and when he spoke, his tone was indignant.

"How dare you! – Just because I forget things now and again. If you knew all that I know, you would forget more than you've ever learned. I didn't forget your name, I just forgot that I know it. That's all."

Eldane was unimpressed. "Will you do as I ask?" he said.

"Oh – alright – just this once mind, but I'm not pleased, you know, not pleased at all. Anyway, what do you want to see?"

"The time of my death – in this world you create."

"I cannot do that."

"Why not?"

"The things I have shown you, could come to pass. No man is permitted to know the time of his death."

"Nonsense! But in any case, you don't have to show me the manner of my death or tell me the exact date. Just a general view, the merest of glimpses will suffice."

Baphomet said nothing but Eldane almost fancied that he saw a scowl appear on his fleshless, crystalline face. The mirror darkened. A man appeared, sitting alone in a bedchamber. He was huge, covered in layers of fat, with bloodshot eyes peering from an ashen, bloated face. With a shock, Eldane recognized the distorted features as his own. The man's breathing was laboured and he sweated profusely. In his hand was a little bejeweled bell, which he rang for attention – but no-one came near. He rang and he rang and as the vision faded, Eldane could still hear the forlorn sound and see his wealthy, powerful self, dying, alone and unloved.

"A wise decision," Baphomet said, as Eldane departed through the left hand door.

Eldane waited in the passageway, allowing Baphomet to catch up. "What can I expect in here?" he asked, nodding towards the door.

"You can expect to be tested," came the cryptic reply. "Pray enter."

Eldane shrugged and did so. The fourth chamber was of, the by now, familiar dimensions, encountered in the others – but this one was empty, almost featureless. Nothing was stored there. Nothing was concealed by curtain or screen. There was only the roughhewn walls, a stone floor and the exit door opposite. Eldane looked at Baphomet quizzically. The skull spoke. "There is a secret contained in this hall," he said. "You must discover it before you leave."

"What kind of secret?"

"That I must not say, but once you have found it, I will tell you more."

Eldane looked around him, right, left, up, down, before and behind. Nothing. He considered for a moment. Was this a trick? Did he merely have to walk on and leave. He decided to try. Traversing the chamber, Eldane came to the exit door – but it did not open at his approach. Putting his shoulder to the door, he pushed but to no avail. He drew his sword and tried to prise an opening, with no greater success. So, there was something else. Eldane felt panic rising but fought it down. He must be patient. Re-crossing the chamber, Eldane began to examine the walls. Slowly and carefully, he worked his way round, peering into every cranny – probing every fissure, pressing every likely looking protuberance. This was taking time and he knew not how much of that was left to spare. Nevertheless, he persevered and at last his perseverance was rewarded. At first, Eldane was uncertain, for the cracks individually looked natural enough – but stepping back, he could discern a pattern. It was the outline, he fancied, of a hidden door – irregular and crooked, to be sure, but a door nevertheless. He pushed, but again nothing happened. Then he saw the ring. It was small, metallic and well concealed. It hung on the door, in what looked like a natural fold in the rock – but now that he saw it, Eldane wondered how he could ever have missed it. Inserting a finger, Eldane tugged and the door swung smoothly open.

"Congratulations," said Baphomet. "You have found the true door. The other was only a decoy – but – I'm afraid there is another problem.

The other problem was beginning to dawn on Eldane. Try as he might, he could not dislodge his finger from the ring. "I'm really sorry," Baphomet said and his voice did sound contrite. "I was not allowed to tell you, before. You see, once that ring closes on flesh, it will never release its hold. I'm afraid you are trapped."

Eldane continued to struggle, his efforts becoming more frenzied. "Help me, Baphomet," he pleaded.

"I cannot."

"But, there must be a way. This is unfair. There has to be an answer. Please Baphomet – guide me."

"There is a way – but you must find it for yourself. I cannot help. I must go on, but will wait for a time in the next chamber. Remember – time runs short."

As if to emphasise his words, the sound of a cock crowing came distinctly to Eldane's ears.

"Surely, it cannot be dawn already," he said – but Baphomet was already gone.

For a moment or two, Eldane tugged and twisted – but could make no difference. He was held fast. There was only one solution that Eldane could see, though he blanched at the idea. "Better to do it now," he told himself. The madness of hunger and thirst would eventually drive him to it anyway – but by then, the quest would be over and Gwyn gone. Awkwardly, he reached to his side and left handed, drew his sword. Steeling himself and trying not to think, Eldane hefted the weapon. "It would have to be my sword hand," he thought aloud. With that thought, his nerve almost failed. For an instant he hesitated but then struck with a blow, swift and true. He was free, but his finger remained trapped. Not daring to look at it, Eldane stumbled from the room. He was halfway along the passageway, when the pain struck, bringing him to his knees, His head spun and almost he swooned. Gathering himself, Eldane managed to cut some cloth from his shirt and used this to staunch the flow of blood. Taking one of his rawhide gaiters, he bound the pad in place and forced himself to stand. With a deep breath, Eldane lurched forward and into the fifth chamber.

Eldane stood for a moment, just inside the threshold, head reeling and body swaying. Then, despite the pain, he grew wary – for this room was full of people. Eldane looked around. He was in a tavern, or so it seemed. Everywhere, people were drinking, some sitting at tables, some standing, some were having conversations with neighbours or the room in general – but most just drank and were silent. Baphomet was nowhere in sight. At the far end, adjacent to the door, was a long trestle table. Behind this, a portly looking individual was filling tankards from a wooden barrel and distributing them to all and sundry. He looked up, noticed Eldane standing there and beckoned. Unsteadily, Eldane moved towards him.

"You look about all in, and fit to drop, if'n I may say so, good sir," said the man, as Eldane approached. "Have a drop of something to revive your spirits, it's on the house, all free, no charges in this establishment."

So saying, he placed a tankard under the spigot and filled it to the brim with amber, foaming liquid. Gratefully, Eldane accepted the vessel and gulped down a long, smooth draught. Almost at once, he began to feel better. A warming glow settled in his stomach and seemed to radiate throughout his body. Already, the pain in his hand was easing. His head cleared and weariness fell from him. Eldane drained the rest of his tankard. This was good. He felt invigorated, ready to go on to the next challenge. Perhaps, just one more draught, before he went. Eldane caught the tapman's eye and signalled for a refill. "Certainly, good sir. It's on the house, all free, no charges in this establishment."

The words seemed familiar to Eldane but he couldn't quite place them. He had raised the tankard to his lips and taken the merest sip, when Baphomet appeared.

"Hail and well met, my old friend," cried Eldane. "Come. Have a drink. It's very good." Then he stopped, embarrassed at the thoughtlessness of his words. He began to apologise but Baphomet cut him off.

"You should know, Eldane, that what you drink is the Mead of Forgetfulness – and it is a powerful brew."

"Is it, indeed?" said Eldane. "It has certainly made me forget the hurt in my poor hand. I feel – I feel wonderful. I even look forward to the next test – whatever it might be."

"Don't you understand, foolish one?" said Baphomet, sternly. "This is the test."

"How so?"

"Did you imagine that this was some kind of charitable hostelry, placed for the benefit of wayfarers, seeking refreshment? Have you learned nothing? In this place, you face great peril – or at least, those relying on you do."

Eldane looked concerned and absent mindedly raised the tankard to his lips.

"I see no peril," he said. "What is the test anyway?"

"You are already half way to failing it," answered Baphomet. "I will explain," he continued. "Listen and understand, if your senses are not already too befuddled." Eldane nodded and took another sip.

"Drink no more Eldane, before you hear me through, for you must again make a choice. You must choose between reality, with all its pains and sorrows, or oblivion. Look around you. These chose oblivion."

Eldane did so and again noticed how most of his companions merely sat drinking, eyes vacant, saying nothing. Even those who spoke, he suddenly realised, were not conversing, but merely saying words, nonsenses, snatches of phrases, out of context and meaningless.

Baphomet continued. "It does not take much of the Mead to make you forget. I caution you, that one sip more may suffice. Then, you will forget your home, your woman, your quest, even your very name. Already, you have done great damage, for having tasted the Mead of Forgetfulness, you will ever after, crave it. Yet, it is not too late. You must choose. Drink no drop more and carry on, or stay here forever – alive in body but dead in all else." Eldane paused, tankard halfway to his lips and tried to ponder Baphomet's words. He found them confusing. The sounds were familiar but somehow he could not always grasp or remember the meanings.

"I go now to the next chamber, the Hall of Judging." Said Baphomet. "I will not wait there long, for if you don't come soon, you will not come at all."

Eldane looked around him, once again. This was strange. Where was he? He seemed to recall speaking to someone, on a matter of some urgency and – although it did not seem so long ago – the subject and the speaker eluded him. He raised the tankard. "How did that happen?" Eldane said aloud, noticing the blood on his hand and the rough binding where his finger should be. He lowered the tankard without drinking and tried to concentrate. Then, began a terrible struggle, more terrible than his fight with Malgrath, in the first chamber – and the outcome was just as uncertain. Memories returned slowly and with great effort – but a determination had grown in Eldane. Whereas before, he might have given up his fight, might even have welcomed oblivion – now he would not. Much depended on him. He remembered the Sword. He remembered the quest. He remembered Baphomet. He remembered Morgan telling him that he had slumbered too long and that he should be up and doing – and he remembered Gwyn. The tankard fell to the floor and he strode from the room, followed by the tapman's endless litany. "It's on the house, all free, no charges in this establishment."

Despite his determination, Eldane had not yet come completely to his senses, so it took him some time to realise that this passage was unlike the rest. It curved to the left and seemed to slope upward. At first, the curve and rise were fairly gentle – but they tightened and steepened as he stumbled on. Eldane began to feel disquiet. The passageway seemed endless and soon, he could only see a short distance ahead or behind. The pain returned in his injured hand, throbbing ever more strongly – and with it, doubts and fears assailed him. Another ache took hold and vied for mastery with that in his hand. He ached for the Mead. His insides felt hollow. There was no substance, no strength, only a burning, seething emptiness. Nothing but the Mead, could salve that gnawing void and make him whole again. Almost, Eldane turned back. He was sweating now, breathing hard – and not only from his exertions. But, still he pressed on. At every moment, his will threatened to crumble and send him careering back whence he had come – but still he held his way. At last, abruptly, the passage levelled and straightened. Eldane stopped. Before him was the entrance to the sixth, or was it the fifth, chamber. He couldn't quite remember. On the door, was carved and painted, a solitary piercing eye – and above it, incised in the wood, were ominous runes. Eldane had never learned letters – but by some power, he understood those before him. Four words only – "This Place Is Terrible," they said, and their import was daunting. The door opened and Eldane went through.

"Welcome to the Hall of Judgement," said Baphomet. Eldane could see that this chamber differed from the rest. It was slightly smaller and the walls were not roughhewn but smooth. From them, came a dim luminescence, barely sufficient to illuminate the interior. In the very centre of the room, stood a chair of simple design and seemingly cut from living crystal, not unlike that which gave Baphomet substance. Facing the chair was a mirror, almost the twin of that used by Baphomet in the Hall of Riches – but this one was silver rather than gold.

"Listen well," said Baphomet. "And I will tell you what must be. From this place, you can go in two directions – on to the Sword Chamber – or back to the Hall of Oblivion – but first, you must be judged. Let me tell you that no-one faces this judgement and emerges unchanged – whether for good or ill. I will depart soon and go on to the Sword Chamber – there to await your coming. It is therefore possible that we may never meet again – for the judge is stern, unrelenting and all-seeing. The judge is you. You will sit on that chair and journey back through time and into your innermost soul. Consider all things carefully, Eldane, for you cannot fool yourself. When you at last arise from the Seat of Seeing, you will either know yourself worthy, or desire only to seek the realms of forgetfulness, drowning your pain in the sea of oblivion. Go now. Take your place – and may Mannan guide and protect you."

With that, Baphomet was gone and Eldane stood alone. Never did he feel less able to undertake any challenge, let alone, the one which faced him now. His body was wracked with pain and his muscles cramped, He felt feverish and light-headed. Fits of trembling seized him from time to time and his legs felt unable to carry him. Agonisingly, he tottered forward, somehow reached the chair and sat down.

A faint hum sprang up around the chamber, grew in strength and settled to a steady drone. The chair began to glow a spectral green – the radiated light catching Eldane and showing his haggard features, in ghastly relief on the silver mirror. "There lies the image of a true hero," he said ruefully and with those words, a wave of defeat, failure and self-pity, washed over him. He dropped his eyes and tried to look away. Suddenly, the chair flared bright, a dazzling, merciless, white light, from which there was no escape. Eldane sat exposed, his features and form reflected in stark detail. He must look. He must see. He must confront himself – face every weakness, every failing, every dark corner of his innermost being. The prospect alone, was enough to bring madness but there was no escape that way either. He must stay and look, until the chair released him from his dire exploration. Then he could seek the refuge of madness or the Mead, but not before. As if to acknowledge his acquiescence, the chair settled back to its previous lesser, but still pervasive glow.

Eldane's mind started questing backwards, beginning with the last chamber and taking each in turn thereafter. In every case, he fancied little cause for satisfaction. Though he had survived and overcome each challenge, it seemed he had been less than worthy, had always made some error in thought or deed. Had only barely scrambled through and had not deserved to do so.

Why had he accepted the tankard of Mead? He should not have done so – should not have been distracted from the quest. The craving and pain he now felt, were self-inflicted, just punishment from his dereliction. He merited no better. Imperceptibly, the light from the chair dimmed a shade and the drone dropped a lower tone. Why had he placed his finger in the ring? Why had he not probed it first with a dagger or sword? Elation – false pride in the empty triumph of his discovery? And having done so, why panic into such drastic action? Perhaps, the ring could have been dislodged from its setting. Perhaps, it could have been severed, instead of his finger. More, deserved mortification. Again, light and sound responded, to Eldane's spirits, dropping depth and intensity. And then, the Hall of Riches – oh yes, he had been tempted. Such wealth! Such power! True, the thought only passed briefly through his mind, but it had been there. And why had he gone through the whole charade with the mirror? All this gained was the loss of precious time. How would he have decided, if he had not suspected some trick, or if the final vision had been different? Eldane was sure none of this had been apparent to Baphomet, but he himself knew – and there was no denying it. There had been no concealing his lust for the woman. He had wanted her, had burned for her. How could he do that? How could he forget the woman he claimed to love, whom he alone could save, in an animal frenzy for that fell creature of the night. Then, there was Malgrath. Yes, he had slain that monster, but if there had been a way of escape, he would have fled, probably screaming in terror. He had fought, only to preserve his miserable life and for no other reason.

Then, Eldane travelled back further – and with each step, the glow from the chair grew ever dimmer and the sound dropped ever deeper. He remembered his fear on the journey. He remembered Morgan's words – and understood. It had been in his power, for years, to do something about his people's plight, but he had done nothing, not even tried. Had the People of Mannan stayed strong and united, The Painted People would never have come. Eldane could have done something, taken, taken some responsibility, but had done nothing. Even Gilmar could have been stopped, should have been stopped, would have to be stopped – if it were not already too late. And then there was Gwyn. She had suffered because of him, but even had Gilmar not perpetrated his foul deed, her fate had been sealed anyway, for the

Painted People had come – and still Eldane did nothing. It had not even been his idea, to ride for the Sword. Morgan had bullied him into the attempt.

Eldane sank lower and lower. His thoughts ceased to flow in any kind of order, but leapt forth and back across an endless vista of blackness and burning shame. He saw himself through the eyes of others and agreed with what they saw. Worse, he saw himself through the window of his own soul and knew what others could not. Failure – coward – worthless – foul – sluggard – the words throbbed in his head – soon ceasing to be words and becoming feelings – concepts more awful than any conferred by language.

The downward spiral continued, agonisingly and relentlessly, until it could go no further. Eldane sat in, all but total, darkness and only a half felt vibration betrayed any sound. As it was without – so it was within. He felt nothing, not even shame. His soul wandered in darkness, had found despair – and had passed even beyond that. Eldane was at the nadir of existence, almost into the void. Of his own volition, had any remained, he might have stayed there, for – was this not oblivion – but the chamber would not allow it. Slowly, it began to bring him back. Now, it seemed to Eldane, that he walked a dark tunnel and could see nothing – but, as he walked, the light grew and the source of that light was himself. A spark had been kindled, or had never died, within him and now it burst forth into flame. The tunnel forked and Eldane knew which way he must go. Soon, he smelt the salt air and heard the restless crash of wave on shore. Ahead was a radiance of dancing blues and greens. Eldane quickened pace, his heart lifting with joy. Before long, he emerged into a cavern filled with the wonderous music of the deep. All around were seashells and corals, crystalised outcrops of salt and multi-hued seaweeds. Two great grey seals frolicked in a deep rock pool – and beside it, stood a man. Eldane could see that his face was calm and serene – but sensed that a wildness and fury resided there, just waiting to be unleashed.

"Welcome, Eldane," said the man. "It pleases me that you have found the way."

"I thank you, My Lord, that you deign to receive me," answered Eldane.

"Then, you know who I am?"

"Yes, Father."

"Tell me quick then and tell me true, Eldane, what you have learned and why you deem your hands worthy to receive my Sword."

Then Eldane spoke, unrehearsed, things that he knew but had not perceived their learning.

"I have learned," he said, "That without fear there cannot be courage, without temptation there cannot be virtue, without defeat there cannot be victory, without sorrow one cannot know joy, without adversity nothing is achieved. I know myself to be only a man, and as such, subject to the failings of men. But, I have faced those failings and now, neither belittle them, nor raise them too high. I accept what I am, but will strive to be better. I was not worthy before. I know not, if I am now, but will try to be."

"Go then, Eldane. Return to your quest. There is yet one more test to face, ere the Sword can be yours. But, if you succeed, remember, that the weapon not only destroys but builds and heals also. Use your stewardship wisely. Do not disgrace your heritage."

Eldane awoke and the pain returned, threatening to overwhelm him. But though his body ached, his spirit was strong. He fought back the pain and forced his rebellious body into motion. Had he been dreaming? It mattered not – he would go on. Was it too late? Had the night long fled? Had he really heard a cock crow? If he had, it seemed like an eternity ago. Maybe days had passed. Maybe Gwyn was gone and the village of Caermannan no more. There was naught else to do, no other hope, one way only of finding the truth. He must win the Sword. Gathering himself, Eldane left the Hall of Judging and stepped directly into the Sword Chamber.

Straightway, Eldane's eyes fell on the Sword – the end of his quest, the legendary Tyr-Mannan. It protruded from a mound of living rock, wherein Mannan had thrust it, with his own hand, long ages ago, when Strivling had been not a hill but an island, standing in a sea, long since departed. Baphomet was there and with him another. Eldane forced himself to remain calm – no easy task, now that the end was in sight.

"Most strange, most strange," said Baphomet – and his voice seemed somewhat agitated. "For centuries, warriors have been coming here, to the Place of Striving – in search of the Great Sword – but all have failed. And now – and now, within moments of each other, it seems two have succeeded. Eldane, meet Mangan. Mangan, this is Eldane."

Eldane regarded the young man and saw that he too was much the worse for wear. His left arm hung limply by his side. Dried blood encrusted his forehead and his eyes were swollen and weary.

"How can this be?" asked Eldane, feeling cheated. "I never encountered him on my way. How came he here?"

That is easily answered," explained Baphomet. "For there are many tests and diverse routes. Each must journey his own path and face his own trials. No two are the same."

"What then is to happen?" demanded Eldane. "For I will not be cheated. I claim my right."

"You have, as yet, earned no right," said Baphomet sternly. "There is one Sword and two of you. Only one can succeed. Only one is ordained to survive the tests. You must fight. For while one yet exists, the other cannot claim the Sword. So it is ordered and so must it be."

"So be it," said Eldane grimly, feeling anger rise in him. His pains were forgotten in the swell of his ire, as he drew his sword and gripped it two-handed. Mangan did not seem so eager for battle but, almost reluctantly, drew his own blade.

I salute you, Eldane," said the young man and his voice was gentle and touched with sadness. "I regret that we should meet thus – one of us to die, after coming so far. If my need was not great and if it were allowed, I would withdraw – but I cannot." He raised his sword in salute and stood ready. Eldane merely grunted and tensed, ready to spring. A moment in time, they stood locked in a motionless tableau, then, with a roar like a lion and the fury of a demon, Eldane attacked. This was no battle, like that with Malgrath, for his opponent could not resist his onslaught. It seemed that Mangan must also have taken a wound – one in his leg, for he limped badly and moved sluggishly. A flurry of blows and the sword went crashing from his hand, as he sank to one knee, in defeat. Eldane raised his weapon high, ready for the killing stroke. Mangan did not flinch, but raised his gaze to Eldane. His features were composed and no fear showed in his eyes. For several heartbeats, they remained thus, like men turned to stone, unmoving, unblinking.

"I will not do this," said Eldane, casting aside his sword. "This man is no enemy of mine. The fight was not even fair. He was too grievously wounded. I will not slay him." He turned away, shoulders slumped and bitterness rising in his throat. To fail now – but what else could he do? He was no butcher – and the man had suffered, just as he had.

"Be of good cheer, Eldane, Keeper of Tyr-Mannan," said a voice behind him. "For you have passed the final test." Eldane whirled round to face his erstwhile opponent and found instead, Velyn – but much changed from last they met. Here, indeed, was the venerable sage, with wisdom in his eyes, clothed in garments of snow, with a golden diadem encircling his flowing, silver hair and noble brow. Eldane's jaw dropped. "Well, this was the way you imagined me," said Velyn, smiling. "I can take many shapes, including the tragic Mangan," and for a moment that is who he was. Then, he was the Sage again. "Think Eldane – could we have entrusted the power of Tyr-Mannan to one with no mercy in his soul? Of course not. Come, draw forth the Sword, for you have earned it."

In a dream, Eldane walked to the mound and laying both hands in the hilt, for it was large, he drew it smoothly from the rock. In an instant, he stood beneath the moon, Sword clasped in both hands with light from Velyn's campfire sparkling along the runes incised on its blade. Before him, was the mound, through which he had entered the chambers and beside him stood Velyn, back in his tatters and matted hair. Eldane turned to the wizard. "How long have I been here?" he asked. "How many nights have passed?"

"Why – You've only just arrived," came the answer, in familiar querulous tones.

Had this all been a dream? But no – he held the Sword. On impulse, Eldane held up his hand, half expecting to see the finger restored, or never having been gone – but he was wrong. The wound was closed and there was no pain but his sword hand was one finger short.

"A small price to pay," said Velyn. "Do not tax your brain, trying to understand. You have walked paths, where few mortals have gone. Time and space run differently there. The Chambers exist – but as much in your soul, as in the Rock. Now then, if I've managed to totally baffle you, it's time to begone."

"Yes, I have work to do," said Eldane, nodding.

Epona brayed a welcome as they approached and trotted over to nuzzle Eldane. Of the She-Wolf, there was no sign, much to his relief. Velyn provided a baldric of rich, red leather studded with brass, so that Tyr-Mannan could be strapped to the bearer's back. It was too long to hang at his belt. Eldane mounted up and listened while Velyn imported a few final words of wisdom.

"Remember, King Eldane," he said "There is a time to kill and a time to heal – a time to destroy and a time to build. Do each, in its due time and you will rule well. Go now, with my blessing – and with Mannan's aid, you will prosper."

Eldane raised his hand in salute. "Why Velyn, you forget yourself," he said. "You sound almost friendly. Give my regards to Baphomet. I'll come back and visit when I'm able." With, that, he gave Epona her head and they were away.

Back down the hill they went, Epona needing no guidance this time. Then they were off again, on their wild gallop – re-crossing carse, field, forest, bog and stream. Eldane had much to think on and he did so, but still found time to marvel at Epona's endurance, for she had but little chance for rest between their journeys. Just before dawn, they breached the ranks of the Painted People yet again – and there was even more panic at their coming this time – for the rumour spread abroad, that Mannan himself had returned to wreak terrible revenge on the invaders. Word passed from mouth to mouth and campfire to campfire. Braver spirits, discounted the story but there was little ease in the hearts of that vast host as they awaited the coming dawn.

Into the village pelted horse and rider, drawing the sleepless inhabitants to door and window, at the noise of their coming. Straightway to Morgan's hut they thundered. Eldane leaped from the saddle whilst Epona was still in full flight – and crashed through the door, almost taking it from its mounting. Morgan turned from her place beside Gwyn, a look of mingled joy and wonder on her face.

"You have returned," she managed to gasp.

Gwyn lay pale and unmoving – almost, it seemed, without breath or life.

"Stand aside, Morgan," said Eldane – and there was an air of quiet authority in his voice. Morgan did as she was bade, sensing something different – a new strength, or maybe an old one rediscovered, in her foster son.

Eldane reached over his shoulder and drew forth the blade. Slowly, he brought it forward, until the tip rested on Gwyn's unmoving breast. A power began to grow in Eldane, charging the very air with its force. He seemed to grow and expand, filling the whole room, yet his physical body remained the same – did not alter. Though men speak of aura or spirit in their ignorance, this was something beyond names and beyond human understanding. This was something elemental. Eldane gathered his strength, as the Thunder God does before unleashing his bolts on the earth below. Then, he too released it, like unseen lightening, through the channel of the Great Sword – and into the body of Gwyn. For a moment, all was still – Eldane was just a man and the room was just a room. Then Gwyn stirred. She breathed. The colour returned to her face and the bruises faded to nothing. Slowly – wonderingly – she sat up.

" I have walked strange roads and been to strange places," she said – her voice sounding dreamy and far away. Eldane re-sheathed the Sword and gently took her hand. He sat beside her on the edge of the bed and spoke her name. The sound of his voice and the touch of his hand, finally drew Gwyn all the way back. With a cry of joy, she embraced him and he her. Then, they were lovers re-united – nothing more, nothing less, as they clung to each other – hot kisses mingling with salt tears – words of endearment, both tender and fierce, spilling from their lips – while they laughed and wept together. In time, their separation had not been long, but the distance had been dire.

At length, Eldane gently but firmly drew apart. "I must go now, my love," he said. "But, soon I'll return." Gwyn was about to speak but he placed a finger on her lips – and she was silent. Then, she noticed his injured hand and again was about to speak – but something stopped her. She recognised the change in Eldane – saw the strength she had always sensed. Before, it had lain hidden – dormant – but now it shone forth and with it came assurance and something else. What that was, Gwyn could not say – but he had grown – was different – had somehow come into his own. She held her peace.

Eldane rose from the bed and Gwyn with him. Together they walked to the door, preceded by an excited and joyous Morgan. Outside, a throng had gathered, drawn by curiosity and perhaps, an unspoken hope. They drew back, as Morgan plunged into their midst, creating space for Eldane.

"Rejoice. Oh Children of Mannan!" she proclaimed. "For the King has returned! All hail King Eldane. He has come at the darkest hour, to bring us hope and destruction to our enemies. Behold! The Great Sword!"

Morgan continued in this vein for some moments, before the meaning of her words reached the understanding of those assembled. At first, people were incredulous, thinking she had been seized by a madness, but then they saw that, which Eldane wore on his back. The pent up fear, desperation and bitterness of recent times, was suddenly swept aside, in a torrent of unsurpassed joy and unhoped for relief. They had a King. He had the Sword. What matter, that the hills were still infested with vast hordes of enemies. The King would conquer. The People would survive and the land would prosper yet again. Once more, Eldane mounted his good and faithful Epona, who alone seemed unmoved by the waves of euphoria that swept the village – and just as dawn broke, rode forth to join the warriors – with the cheers of the women, children and old men, ringing in his ears.

To the north of the village, the pitifully few warriors of Mannan, sat their mounts on the hilltop and wondered at the clamour coming from their homes. Had the village already been attacked? But no – those were not the voices of warriors – and the tone was joyous. All around, the Painted People too heard the acclaim – and were uneasy.

Soon, the warriors of Mannan could see a lone horseman approaching – and they also grew uneasy – some more than others – for something seemed to flow from that solitary figure. Some sensed great power – others, a terrible wrath. A few, perceived only death and oncoming destruction. In hushed voices, those with the sharpest eyes, identified the newcomer.

"It is Eldane," they said and knew not why his coming should be so portentous. Only one among them, remained undaunted, or at least seemed to – though the blood did drain from his face – he who should have feared most – Gilmar.

When Eldane grew close, Gilmar put spur to his horse and rode forward to meet him.

"What brings you here, Brother?" asked Gilmar, his tone arrogant.

"I have come for you – that the world might be a cleaner place," answered Eldane.

"Why, such courage," mocked Gilmar. "Can this be Eldane – the skulker? Eldane the ditch digger? Eldane come to die like a man? Surely not? It must be some other in his guise." Eldane said nothing but dropped his reins and drew forth the Sword. A sound, somewhere between a gasp and a groan ran round the watching warriors. Even Gilmar's mocking arrogance misgave him for a moment, but he recovered and drew his own weapon.

"I see you have a new toy," he smirked. "Well, I can take that as easily as I took your other plaything." As the last word escaped his lips, Gilmar attacked. He spurred ahead, bearing down on Eldane, his sword already arcing forward, in a killing stroke. Eldane had no time to react, no time to dodge or parry, but Tyr-Mannan was thirsty. In Gwyn, the Sword had pulled a soul back from the void's very brink. Now, another must take her place. The Sword thirsted for battle, thirsted for blood, thirsted for Gilmar. Faster than the eye could follow, Tyr-Mannan turned in Eldane's hand, biting through flesh, bone and harness as Gilmar impaled himself, almost to the very hilt. The Sword drank deeply, holding Gilmar still in the saddle, till his life ebbed away. Then, he crashed to the ground and the blade came free. With the Sword still held in both hands, Eldane urged Epona forward with a gentle pressure of his knees. All was confusion, as warriors dismounted, to fall on one knee, in homage to their rightful King. None doubted that, though some, with good reason, knew dread at the prospect. For a moment, Eldane surveyed them, his face impassive – masking the turmoil and conflict he felt inside. Part of him cried out for vengeance against the guilty, but he himself had been culpable before. "A time to kill and a time to heal – a time to destroy and a time to build." He was King now. More than a man and less than a man. Personal considerations must give way to the greater good. It was time to heal the Children of Mannan – time to build anew.

"Warriors!" he cried. "Arise. Henceforth, no man will kneel to any other. Arise and remount!" As they did so, all eyes were drawn down the sloping ground and a chill touched many hearts, for the Painted People had finally come to battle. Like a vast sea of living bodies, they seethed and swarmed up the hill. Their spears were like a forest and the ground trembled at the thunder of their feet.

"Warriors of Mannan!" cried Eldane. "To-day I lead you into battle, but before we go to victory or to death, you must swear me an oath. Any, who will not do so, must ride forth and seek escape or death, as best they can. All transgressions before this day, are pardoned – but never again, must any stand by, whilst the innocent suffer. So now, you must swear by Mannan, to protect the oppressed, champion the weak and succour the innocent. With one voice, the warriors roared, "We swear, by Mannan!"

The fierceness of their cry, gave pause to their advancing enemy, who, in truth, had been unsettled by the rumours and events of the past night. They were a savage, superstitious race, who feared the darkness and peopled it with creatures of nightmare. By now, however, they saw how few stood against them and their courage waxed strong. On they came, laughing and prancing, in primitive insult to their foes.

King Eldane put himself at the head of his men and held the Great Sword aloft. Suddenly, as if in answer to a signal, a sound fit to chill the blood echoed high and clear, around the field of battle. Like the baying of some hell-hound, it hung in the air, before stopping, to leave an even more terrible silence. Consternation seized the Painted People. Already, they feared the Sword. They could sense its power, though ignorant of its history. Then, from the trees, burst a creature of nightmare indeed. It bounded up the hill to the King's side, red eyes blazing and jaws slavering with anticipation. Drawn by the Sword and sensing slaughter, the She-Wolf had come to the feast.

Panic took the Painted People – for surely Mannan had indeed returned and brought his hound, Hrymer, to the battle. They sought to flee, caring nought where they ran. Weapons were cast away and those who stumbled were trampled underfoot. Then, King Eldane, led his men forth and the slaughter began. No battle was this, for no fight was left in the Painted People. The warriors of Mannan rode among them like grim reapers in a field of wheat – and great was their harvest. Never again, would the Painted People dare to cast their eyes towards Eldane's kingdom – for their power was broken that day, beyond recovery.

So it was, that Eldane became King and set about freeing his kingdom. And under his rule, the kingdom prospered and grew even larger, until it became an Empire and he an Emperor. His conquests were not all by the sword – for his fame was great and he brought justice wherever he went. Oppressed peoples would turn to him at need and he would champion their cause. Gwyn became Queen – then Empress – and together they founded a Dynasty. Neither did Eldane forget his promise to Velyn – for he visited Strivling whenever he could. He renewed his acquaintance with Baphomet, who eventually came to reside with him and be his advisor. The reign of Eldane Nine Fingers was a golden age indeed. He lived long, ruled well and was happy, though in times of sorrow – which even kings must have – his thoughts oft turned to the Mead of Forgetfulness – and the craving returned.

But always, the Wheel turns and Eldane, being mortal, finally departed this world. He was nothing loath to go, for Gwyn had gone ahead of him, two winters before and he longed to be with her again. The Great Sword was consigned to the deep on his death – for it was not an heirloom but merely on loan. It is gone from the world of men now – but should the need arise, I'm sure Mannan will find someone worthy to draw if forth from wherever it now rests. But for now, my tale must end and I will accept what hospitality you may wish to offer. If it is pleasing, I may remain another night and speak of other things. If not, I'll depart and find a place wherein my value is appreciated as much as I myself appreciate it.

The Gauntlet.

I'll always remember the day that me and my squadmates at Station 17 made "Million Coin Gauntlet" history. It was Trumpvember 30th 2073, the last day of the Summer Season. That was my rookie year. You younger folk won't realise how huge "Gauntlet" was back then. For fifteen years it topped Global Teleview Network's ratings – up until the Neo-Puritans took over the World Government and banned it. They strait-laced bastards hate anyone having fun. Gauntlet was the brainchild of another political party – The Bread and Circuses Party, who were in Government at the time. They also are outlawed now.

Gauntlet was created with mass entertainment very much in mind. Every aspect of it was covered by cameras. Even sniper's bullets carried a minute devices on their tip – showing the projectile's journey "from barrel to brain." I was one of two "pom-pom" gunners in the match squad. We did most of the heavy lifting, taking out the vast majority of the onrushing vehicles. Ours was bludgeoning work – little finesse but maximum carnage. My numbers were great that season. Besides us, there were four snipers, equipped with precision weapons, capable of long and short range work. But the star of every squad was the swivel gunner. This was who every kid wanted to be. There was only one per squad, armed with a heavy-duty, swivel mounted, rapid firing machine-gun. This was the backstop. They did all the mopping up and last-minute saves over the last half mile. Just about everything they did was fraught and exciting.

Anyone with a motor vehicle could enter the Gauntlet. The object was to survive a three mile dash, under the fire of the defenders' gun squad. Some competitors, the ones with the least resources, used standard cars and vans – but most serious entrants had custom made vehicles. The debate was always between speed and armour. The more protection carried, the slower the speed. Getting that balance right was crucial – but the driver also had to have, nerve, skill and top-level physical co-ordination. The prize for reaching the tunnel at the end of the road, was one million coin – a veritable fortune. It was a way out of poverty and the keys to a new life. Failure, meant a violent and messy death.

Let me describe the general set up. Most of you will probably never have seen a Gauntlet run. There were 24 stations worldwide and we ran four seasons yearly (Spring, Summer, Fall and Winter). A season ran for fifteen consecutive days. Starting at 9am, each station would stage a run, one after another – two in every hour. The run itself was quite straight forward. There was a klaxon sounded to begin the match and, twenty minutes later, another to end it. Contestants had to reach the tunnel before that final klaxon, to qualify for the prize. The run-road was exactly three miles long and straight. At the start line, the road was half a mile broad. This narrowed uniformly, over the first mile, to one hundred yards. It stayed that way for the remaining two miles. The tunnel entrance itself was a mere thirty yards wide. The Swivel-Gunner was positioned on a platform, suspended twenty feet above this.

The competitors were parked up in a holding area, out of sight of the guns. From this, there were fifty slip roads leading to the start line. When the first klaxon sounded, the competitors could choose their moment to enter the fray. Various tactics were employed. Some judged that being part of a mass influx, early in proceedings, was the way to go. They hoped that their odds of survival would be better, given so many targets for the guns to go after. Others delayed until near the end of the gauntlet. At speed, it didn't take long to traverse the three miles. The longer you delayed your run, the more wreckage would be strewn around. This worked in two ways. It meant there were more obstacles to be avoided but these self-same obstacles could also provide cover, if used judiciously. So – to win the prize, you had to survive the three miles of mayhem and carnage, under constant gunfire and attain the safety of the tunnel. All who achieved this won the prize. There could be multiple winners in any Gauntlet, each of whom received the fabled million coin. It demanded great driving ability, icy courage and an inordinate slice of luck to succeed. Still – there was never any shortage of entrants. Given the prevalent poverty of the time, it was the only way to riches for the prole underclasses.

So, back to Trumpvember 30th 2073. There was great excitement, all around the world. None of the twenty four stations had ever achieved the fabulous "Slam". This entailed going through a whole season without any of the contestants getting "Home". No station had ever even come close. But now, with one Gauntlet to go, we at Station 17 were on the verge of doing it. For fourteen consecutive runs, no-one had managed to evade our guns. After we passed Gauntlet number ten if began being spoken of. Each run after that, the hysteria and pressure ramped up. We tried to remain calm and professional but one careless or unlucky slip – and the holy grail could be dashed from us. All the talk shows focused on it. The hype was tremendous – and growing daily. The world held its breath. The broadcast schedules were redrawn, so that our final Gauntlet would be the last one to be run that day. It was to be the grandest of grand finales for the Summer Season.

As each station did its season's final run throughout the day, the hype and hysteria grew. We all had to do several interviews with the networks, where we were quizzed about the possibility of completing the first ever "Slam" and what it meant to us. It was not the best preparation for such an important sporting event, but we had to comply with our contractual obligations. Finally, with just over an hour to go, we were left alone to get our heads together. Our names are lost to history now, but for a while, we were the most famous humans on the planet. Wearing our station's famous blue and silver jumpsuits that day were, Snipers: Tom Addison – Gordon Cooper – Joan Hynd – Ken Wilkie. Pom-Pom Gunners: Jim Forrest – Mick Carey (me). Swivel Gunner: Frances Clink. Frances was undoubtedly the star of the show. She was a tall gorgeous blond, who wore the most tight-fitting jumpsuit. Her performance could almost have been choreographed. She embodied deadly accuracy and lethal concentration, wrapped up in graceful body form and movement. She loved the camera and the camera loved her.

So, with fifteen minutes to go, we took up our positions. The guns had been fully tested a bit earlier by our technicians. We settled in and did our pre-game rituals. Every gunner had one. They were ostensibly a way of focusing our minds. In reality, they owed just as much to superstition as to psychology. They brought us luck. The five minute warning sounded in our earbuds and we wished each other "good shooting." The squad were all miked up. We could speak to each other but everything we said was broadcast immediately to the watching world. There was a language code. Certain words were forbidden. In case any of us let one slip out in the heat of the moment, there was an automatic bleeper to protect the sensitive ears and sensibilities of our audience. Privately, we mocked this amongst ourselves. People were getting mangled into bloody messes, right in front of their eyes, but they'd be shocked by the word sh*t.

It was normal to feel pre-game nerves but for this one my stomach was in a knot and my heart was pounding. Presumably, my squadmates were the same. Then the klaxon sounded. The waiting was over and it was down to business. Straightaway, we were hit with the customary initial stampede. Vehicles poured down the many slip-roads and sped towards us. The theory was that this would catch the gunners cold, before we got our eye in. Plus – the sheer number of targets might overwhelm us. No-one seemed to realise that this was rarely successful. Occasionally, someone would scrape through but not very often. Ironically, this opening rush actually helped us. The sheer hectic action settled our nerves and it was like shooting fish in a barrel – particularly for us pom-pom gunners. We couldn't fire a shot without hitting something.

Pom-pom gunners were housed in rotating turrets on either side of the road. There were four cannons, mounted in a square configuration, two above and two below. The name came from the noise made when continuously firing. The top two discharged (pom) followed closely by the bottom two (pom) – and so on. The shells we used, exploded on contact and we could inflict rapid and extensive carnage – and that is exactly what we did that day. Cars exploded into flying shards and these, in turn inflicted death on those around them. Many died in that opening onslaught. Bloody, body parts intermingled with the hurtling, death dealing debris. Out of control vehicles smashed into others and formed unpassable walls of wreckage. Within a few minutes, the initial rush was mauled to a stop. Our rapid-fire snipers finished off drivers trapped in their ruined motors and cut down any who tried to flee on foot. The multi-camera broadcast showed all this in intimate close-up and replayed the best ones in loving slow motion.

With it being the last Gauntlet of the season, the road itself was not in the best of shape. There had been efforts to repair the worst of the damage inflicted by projectiles and exploding vehicles – but fair wear and tear was an accepted part of the event. This did give us an advantage as it was a further complication for our opponents. The match followed the same pattern as most others. There were sporadic surges and individual dashes – all of which we mopped up with consummate ease. Only two vehicles made it far enough for Frances to finish off with her swivel-gun. This she did with her customary panache. The much vaunted and anticipated event looked likely to be a bit of a damp squib. We could still achieve the mythical "Slam" and we'd have been happy with that – but it would have been nice to do it with a bit of style and excitement. We could always put a spin on it – that it showed how proficient we were at our job – but it would undoubtedly tarnish our achievement. Still – the history books would show that Station 17 went a whole season without a score against us. We'd be the first to do so and we'd settle for that.

The bell went off on my earbuds, telling us that there were only five minutes to go. I've got to admit, I was suddenly nervous again. We were so close and I'd settle for a damp-squib shutout. But that wasn't to be. About a dozen vehicles descended the slip-roads and erupted onto the main road. They were moving fast and began weaving zig-zag patterns. It looked like a concerted effort – drivers working together in the hope that at least one would make it through. We went to work again. I quickly took one out and another two fell to our snipers. We pounded away but these guys were good. The rest of them were progressing rapidly. I swivelled frantically and managed to obliterate another one. Jim, on the other pom-pom nailed another. Two of the vehicles zigged when they should have zagged and smashed into each other. Another one hit a deep shell-hole and pulled its front wheels off.

The remaining four were only about half a mile out. A sniper took another one. While we were distracted by this threat, three more vehicles joined the Gauntlet. These were something we hadn't seen before. They were small, only large enough to accommodate a driver and no more – but they ran on four wheels, which is all they had to do to qualify. They got a good head start on us, as we had let ourselves be drawn in by the previous wave. Joan was first to spot the newcomers. She yelled a warning and we turned our attention to them in consternation. We simply had to trust that Frances would deal with the three remaining vehicles, now bearing down on the tunnel. Frances did indeed take care of them. She hosed all three of them in one graceful and lethal movement. Two of them smashed into each other as their drivers died. The third one slewed sideways and came to a halt broadside on to the road, about fifty yards short of the tunnel.

Meanwhile, the three small buggies were eluding our best efforts to blast them. They were very fast and manoeuvrable – and the drivers knew their business. Our "Slam" began to look in doubt. One of our snipers managed to wing a driver. It wasn't a killshot but it was enough for him to lose momentum and I blew him away before he could regain control. That still left two. There was a bright yellow one and the other was black. They were now on the final approach to the tunnel and behind the pom-pom guns. We were out of play. Joan managed to squeeze off one last shot, before the snipers too were out of the game. It was a dream kill. The driver of the yellow vehicle's head exploded. It was now a straightforward one on one – black buggy against Frances and her swivel-gun.

The driver of the black buggy was clever. He used the bulk of the vehicle slewed across the road as a shield. He was too low to the ground for Frances to get a sufficient downward angle to nail him. Her bullets didn't have the power to penetrate the derelict vehicle and do damage. It was all a matter of guesswork now. The buggy had to choose to go left or right to clear the wreckage. If Frances picked the wrong option, the buggy would have a straight sprint for the tunnel. It was all down to her intuition – and she got it wrong. There was thirty seconds left on the clock. So near and yet so far. The buggy veered right and Frances had chosen the other side. There was no way for her to get her gun round in time to get off a final burst. The "Slam" was doomed. That's when fate took a hand. The buggy hit a patch of spilled fuel, skidded at high speed and spun out of control. The driver almost managed to get his vehicle moving again but Frances had lightening reflexes. She spun and blew him away, twenty yards short of safety.

It was all over and we'd done the "Slam". We were jubilant and whooping like crazy people. There was a big slice of luck – but them's the breaks. We'd done it. There was a massive celebration that night and we were feted worldwide. Over the years, the "Slam" was achieved twice more – but we did it first and no-one could take that away from us. The near success of the small nippy buggies, encouraged many more people to try that route to the prize. Sometimes they won – but gunners were ready for them now and the element of surprise was gone. Station 17 never reached those heights again. I managed another three years on the pom-pom but my numbers hovered around average and I was eventually replaced by a brighter prospect. Still – on that late Trumpvember night, my squadmates and I were top of the world.

Killer Krew.

It was a lovely night, mild and clear. As midnight approached, James and Gerry stalked the lone woman. So far, all was going better than could have been expected. They had managed to cut her off from the more populated part of town. In his pocket, James had a Vipertek stun gun, that Big Mick had somehow acquired, but it looked like they might not even need it. The two men had maneuvered the woman onto the footpath that led to the underpass they had scouted earlier. It went under the railway line and was suitably secluded. Big Mick and his girlfriend Maisie waited there, along with Jacko. James had texted them to let them know there was a fish on the hook.

This would be their fourth kill and James thought they were definitely getting better at it. The first one, up in Newcastle, had been a bit underwhelming. That women hadn't lasted long enough. Shagging a corpse wasn't as much fun as a body that was alive and kicking. Their technique had got better over the next two. The last one had been brilliant – everything they could have asked for. James thought, with admiration, of Maisie's contribution that night. Some of the things she'd done to that woman were outrageous but so entertaining to watch. She seemed to enjoy the cruelty, even more than her male companions. James had the hots for Maisie. At nineteen years old, she was pretty and sweet looking on the outside but that just masked the demon within. She was a terror. James had often speculated how Maisie would react to being subjected to the tortures they had inflicted on their victims. She'd probably spit in your eye and tell you to try harder. He would never try anything with her though. She'd have your balls – and if she didn't, Big Mick certainly would. He was one scary dude. That was one relationship definitely made in Hell.

James was relishing the hunt. Tonight promised to be memorable. Their quarry was a good-looking brunette, maybe late twenties or early thirties. It had been just over a week since their last night of fun. They fully intended to have many more. The cops would know by now that they were dealing with serial killers. They'd left plenty of DNA evidence on their victims – and the words "KILLER KREW" carved into their bodies would also alert police to what they were facing. They didn't fear being caught though. They lived completely off-grid, in Big Mick's camper van – which wasn't registered to him. Most, if not all, of them, were likely on a DNA data base somewhere. The cops would have to find them first and that wouldn't be easy. They ranged far and wide –

never striking more than once in any geographical area. With luck, their spree of torture, rape and murder could go on for a very long time.

James and Gerry had been scoping the area for a suitable victim. They had struck gold. A good-looking young woman, out walking alone late at night, was exactly what they were looking for. The two men looked like villains – which wasn't surprising given that, that's exactly what they were. They had menaced the woman, making it clear that they were aware of her and looking as ruffianly as they possibly could. She had two choices. She could try to brazen it out and just push past them – or she could choose to go the other way and hope they wouldn't follow. She chose the latter, which is exactly what the men wanted. It would take her through the underpass – and into the arms of the rest of the Killer Krew. Of course – had she chosen the first option, they would simply have incapacitated her with the stun-gun. Between them, James and Gerry could have manhandled her to the underpass. As it was though, she had saved them the effort. She would make her own way to what awaited her.

They were getting close to the underpass now. The woman must be in a state of anxiety, if not fear. Several times she'd looked back over her shoulder and her heart must have quailed to see that the two men were still following her. It was time to chivy her a bit closer – just in case she tried to breakaway across country. James and Gerry closed the distance between them. As they raised their pace, so did she. Soon she would start to run but it would be too late. James had been keeping the others informed by text and they'd be waiting.

The woman entered the dimly lit underpass and her two stalkers broke into a trot. They reached the entrance of the underpass, just as the other three members of the Killer Krew stepped out to confront the hapless woman. She was all alone, with no way out. The woman stopped, at bay. She surveyed the entire gang and then asked, "So, what happens now?" Maisie laughed and gave an evil grin. "Now we have some fun," she replied. "That's what I thought," the woman said – and she smiled.

* * * * * * * * * * * *

As DCI Donnie Williamson approached the crime scene, his sergeant, Harry Watson came to meet him. "It's a bad one, boss," he said grimly. For the normally stoic Watson to be affected, it must be bad indeed. It was an overcast morning and there was a slight drizzle in the air. The remains had been found by an early-morning jogger. There had been a report, the night before, of screaming – a lot of screaming – but the location had been unclear and a cursory investigation had found nothing. It seemed clear that the location had now been found.

They reached the underpass. It looked like the walls had been painted with blood. They were almost totally covered. There were body parts strewn all over the place. It was a nightmarish scene of carnage. A police photographer was busy taking pictures and the pathologist was crouched in among the scattered remains. He noticed Williamson's approach and stood up. The pathologist, Joe Parke, walked carefully out of the underpass and came to meet the two detectives. They couldn't enter crime scene until he released it to them. Parke was looking pale. "Got a ciggie, Donnie?" he asked. Williamson took a pack from his pocket, gave Parke one and took another for himself. Watson didn't smoke. Donnie flicked his lighter and lit both cigarettes. "Didn't know you smoked, Joe," he said. "Stopped fifteen years ago," Parke replied. "But I need one today."

They smoked in silence for a couple of minutes and then Parke said, "I've found five heads. We won't know for certain until all the body parts have been re-assembled, but I'd say that's how many dead are in there." "What killed them?" Watson asked. "Could it have been a gang fight?" Parke didn't answer for a moment or two. "No. I don't think so," he eventually said. "I haven't seen anything indicating weapon marks. The bodies have been torn to pieces. If there'd been any signs of a blast, I'd have said it was a bomb – but there's none. I don't know what could have done this. Maybe a rabid bear – but we'd have heard about that by now. There's not a lot of bears around here." He gave a humourless laugh. "I simply don't know, he went on. "I've never seen anything like this. Maybe when I've had more time, I'll come up with something." He finished his cigarette and went back to work.

Joe Parke never did come up with a viable explanation. His best guess was an animal attack – but what kind of animal, he couldn't say. It would have to have been something big and very powerful. Such a beast couldn't have gone long unnoticed in the English countryside. He did come up with one concrete conclusion though. DNA testing identified the five mangled corpses as the infamous Killer Krew. Something had got to them before the police did. They wouldn't be killing anymore.

The Munagwyn.

The Gowan Hill, people call it and that's where the Goblins live – only they aren't really Goblins and it isn't really a hill. What they are, I don't really know. They call themselves The Munagwyn, but they look like Goblins and act like Goblins – so that name will do well enough for me. Their home looks for all the world like a hill. It lies below Stirling Castle, to the east and is grass covered, like the true Gowan Hills, which it adjoins. The old Beheading Stone stands on its dome shaped summit, embedded in a plinth of concrete and protected by a cage of iron bars. Beside it are two cannons from some old war – Napoleonic, I think. There used to be a flagpole too, but it's gone now. Yes, everyone in Stirling knows "The Gownie" but not many know that it's man made. A vitrified fort they call it (I looked it up in a book) an ancient stronghold, made by heating rocks until they melt together. There's quite a few of them in Scotland but nowhere else in the world, as far as I know. Men made it but they're long gone now. Only The Munagwyn remain. How do I know this? Well, you won't believe me. Nobody does. I know, because I've been inside.

Before I tell you about my adventure, let me say some more about The Munagwyn. This is what they told me, so it's straight from the Goblin's mouth, you might say – although they are such frightful fibbers that the whole thing might just be one big lie. I don't think, even they, know where they came from in the beginning but they've been living in the Hill since dates were B.C.. They like places where nasty things have happened. You know – human sacrifices, murders, battles and things like that. So, apparently, the vitrified fort suited them very well, because all those things happened there. There were even executions – but that was a long time after they moved in – back in the days when the beheading stone wasn't only an ornament for tourists to look at. Anyway, when the Munagwyn drove out the fort's human inhabitants, they let it fall into disrepair, so that it became overgrown and hill like. People were wiser in those days and avoided the Hill, like it was a Gateway to Hell, which was probably very perceptive of them.

Years passed and men forgot. The Munagwyn went about their business undisturbed, delving long tunnels deep in the earth, staying hidden from view and waylaying people for sport and feasting. They don't really prefer the taste of human flesh to other meats. It's just the idea they like. It's the same with their fondness for torture. It doesn't have any deep religious or social significance. They just enjoy it and do it surpassingly well.

Very clever and adaptable race, The Munagwyn. They move with the times, one might say and they have some remarkable talents. For instance, they can look like and sound like any person they want to. Not that they really change physically, mind you. They just make you think you're seeing what they want you to see. Better than invisibility – eh? They like that – disguises and things. Their tunnels stretch for miles, with secret gateways all over the country. They had a bit of a scare, a few years ago, when the motorway was being built behind Stirling Castle and the excavations nearly unearthed one of their main tunnels – but they've taken precautions since then.

So, what are the Munagwyn doing nowadays. Well, basically the same as they've always done – with some refinements. Accidents – fatal ones, give them some mild amusement. They'll do things like fire raising, tinkering with aircraft instruments and rewiring railway signals – but these are looked upon as mere childish pranks. Murder is better, especially the real gruesome ones. But best of all, is abduction. Then, they can have all the time they want with their victims. It also improves the atmosphere Underhill, they will tell you. But surely, these disappearances would eventually give the Munagwyn away, I hear you say – but you'd be wrong. Remember, there are never bodies to be discovered – at least not up until recently – so murder isn't always suspected. Sometimes they select victims that no-one will ever miss – tramps, runaways and so on. Other times, they'll be even more devious. The victim's family will receive a letter or postcard, written in their loved one's handwriting. Or they'll get a telephone call and recognize the voice. Or someone will spot the victim safe and well, in a neighbouring town. Only, as you've already guessed, it's the Munagwyn doing all this. Everyone thinks that the victim is still alive and might come home someday – everyone except the Munagwyn. They like that, you know. It prolongs the agony for the victim's family and the Munagwyn just love human agony.

The tunnels run far and wide and rarely will the Munagwyn strike in the vicinity of their own doorstep – but there are exceptions. I am one such – doubly so. I alone have looked on the true faces of the Munagwyn and returned from Underhill to tell the tale.

My parents moved from Glasgow to Stirling when I was ten years old and I fell in love with the place right off. I adored the old places – The Castle, The Kirk of The Holy Rude, The Guildhall – but most of all, I loved the Back-Walk and The Gowan Hills. I was a lonely child and didn't make friends easily. I didn't have many in Glasgow and the effort of finding new ones in Stirling, was beyond me. Besides, I never really liked children – even when I was one myself. I preferred being alone, and up The Back Walk, I could be. Let me explain, in case you've never been to Stirling. The Back Walk is a pathway, leading round The Castle and on to the Gowan Hills. It starts off opposite the library, as a kind of lane which climbs directly uphill on the north-western edge of Stirling Rock. On your right, is the old town wall and other buildings. To the left, you look over part of modern Stirling. As you get higher, you can see the King's Knot below. The Cup and Saucer, the locals call it. It's a kind of earthwork thingy, that some people think was King Arthur's Round Table. One legend says that Arthur is sleeping there with all his Knights in Armour. If they are, I bet The Munagwyn have found them. I wonder if they like tinned meat.

Anyway, once you reach the top, you can turn right past the graveyard to the Castle's gate. But my favourite part is to the left – The High Back Walk. This is a pathway, no more than four or five feet broad, that loops round the back of the Castle. It's quiet there. Above you, the Castle perches on its northern precipice, screening off most of the modern town. Below, is the green of farmlands and the King's Park and the straight black ribbon of the Dumbarton Road. The motorway cuts across there now but it does nothing to enhance the view. To be sure, a few minutes further on, the town encroaches once more, and you're looking down on the Raploch housing scheme, but by now, you're swinging back towards The Gowan Hills. The hills sweep down from the Castle, cut only by The Pass of Ballengeich, until they reach my favourite spot, The Gownie. It stands like a knobby doorstop at the very end of the hills – with its beheading stone, cannons and a couple of wooden benches. Did I tell you, there used to be a flagpole there too?

All during my childhood, I would wander these parts alone, sometimes playing truant from school to do so. On through my teenage years and into manhood, I never tired of being there. I never considered it to be a dangerous place. It was certainly isolated, in a half-hearted sort of way, but in reality, the town was all around. Summer, winter, day or night, you'd find me there whenever I got the chance. But nights were best. At night, it was more mysterious, more secluded, as many a courting couple might attest. At night, you could stand on The Gownie, shrouded in a cloak of darkness and look down on the town, exposed and somehow made vulnerable by the streetlighting.

It was about six months ago, I met the Goblins. A shadow had fallen on the town. People were disappearing at an alarming rate. Five, I think it was, in the space of two months. Dark rumours abounded. Someone or something was stalking the Gowan Hills. It was ridiculous really. There was no proof that any of the disappearances had taken place anywhere near there, but that is the way with rumours. It did not deter me. Most nights would still find me in my favourite place.

I remember it well – in parts. The moon was high, bathing everything in silver light and I was alone, atop The Gownie. It wasn't quiet, for the traffic sounds rose to where I stood but, although clear, they seemed somewhat remote, from another world. The sound of low voices startled me and for a moment, I froze. They were coming from a shallow gully, where The Gownie meets the rest of the hills. Silently, I padded across and peered down, keeping myself hidden from view. I couldn't help but chuckle to myself. A young couple, anxious to be alone, had braved the hills that night and were settling down in a grassy hollow, screened from sight to anyone without my vantage point. Then there was another sound – but behind me this time. It was very faint, like a bolt being drawn. I whirled round and I think I gasped. The plinth on which the beheading stone sits, must weigh at least a couple of tons and is embedded firmly in the ground, but the whole thing was tipping sideways, as if on hinges.

I must have been too stunned to move or something, because I watched the trapdoor open completely, without making any attempt to run away. Then, it was too late. The Goblins were upon me. They spewed forth from that black hole, like a drain overflowing and swarmed towards me, gibbering and leering as they came. Half man size, they were but squat and exceedingly strong. If God acknowledges such creatures, then he alone knows how many vomited from the bowels of the hill, to seize me and carry me below. I don't think I cried out or even struggled. It was all too fast and in any case, terror had rendered me immobile.

Down, down they took me into the cold, dank darkness. I can't tell you anything of that wild journey, because my memory of it has been wiped clean by fear. They brought me before their Chieftain, a hideous brute who stood almost as tall as myself. I collapsed at his feet, in a quivering jelly of mortal terror. Then reason began to claw its way back, from wherever it had chosen to flee. The chieftain was talking and giving me to understand that I was not to be harmed – but would be returned presently above ground. I confess, it took some time for this message to sink through – and even longer for me to begin to believe it. It's funny really. The first thing I was conscious of was that he used modern English with a Scottish accent, not unlike mine – this before I even managed to heed the words he was saying. Eventually, I listened and calmed down – but only a little.

I can't say they treated me kindly, for that quality is totally outside their capacity – but, by their standards, I was hospitably received. They gave me food and drink and the Chieftain told me a little about his people – that which I've already related to you. Then, he got round to my unwilling visit to their environs. They had had their eyes on me for some time, he told me. They appreciated my kindred spirit, as shown by my frequent excursions in the neighbourhood of their dwelling – but enough was enough. Undue attention, must not be brought to bear on their locality – lest discovery should ensue. My excursions would have to stop. I didn't know their fondness for human flesh, when they served the refreshments and was unaware what I was eating – besides which, I'd never tasted it cooked before.

They put me to sleep then and took me aloft. That's when the police found me. They'd had a tip-off, anonymous, of course. It didn't take them long to discover the graves, beside a disused path amongst the trees, about half a mile from The Gownie – because, that's where The Munagwyn had left me. I suppose I did get a bit greedy, doing five in two months. Up till then, it had only been one or two a year. Altogether, the police found twenty-seven graves. I swear, only nineteen of them were mine but The Munagwyn must have their little joke – and why not? I've got one too. They'd be fuming to know, they saved two human lives. That young couple will never know how lucky they were.

So here I am – criminally insane. You don't believe me? Neither did the police or the judge. The Munagwyn knew that would happen, of course. When I see that Chieftain again, I'll spit right in his little piggy eye. Oh yes. I'll see him again. They'll be coming for me. I don't know when but they'll be back. Nobody ever escapes The Munagwyn.

KILL THEM ALL!

Ewan Lambert was a sad and bitter man. He would probably have told you that he was broken. His old life hadn't been perfect but it had been alright. It had taken, what he saw as, a perfect storm of circumstances to rob him of it. At first, he'd been merely overwhelmed. He felt hollowed out and empty and missed his wife, child and step-children. Approaching forty, his career was over. Ewan was devastated. All this had happened back home in Fife, four months previously – but now he was living in Essex with his Godmother – his Auntie Fiona. Ewan had been kind of bounced into this. His Mother had thought it would be good for him to make a fresh start – and he'd let himself be persuaded. With the passage of time, thoughts had percolated in Ewan's mind and that's when the bitterness emerged and the dreams had started. He saw clearly now, that three women had done the dirty on him. They were the true authors of his misfortune.

It was in the autumn of 1989, that the haunting began in an innocuous but puzzling fashion. Lambert was living a facsimile of real life. He was basically going through the motions. To others, it looked like he was functioning well enough, but inside, nothing registered as being of any real importance. His cousin, Jeff, had got him a job at a local garage, where he himself worked. Jeff was a mechanic. Ewan's job was petrol pump attendant. It was hardly demanding work, but it gave him money in his pocket and something to occupy him during the day. Every evening, he went to the pub with his Uncle Pat and cousin, Jeff. It was only for the last hour and only a few drinks were taken but it seemed to be a kind of ritual.

So that was the household Lambert joined – Auntie Fiona, Uncle Pat and Cousin Jeff. Auntie Fiona was heavily involved in the Spiritualist Church. She was a trance medium. Ewan reckoned she was quite talented but not above a bit invention. She described one reading she'd given someone to him. He immediately recognized it as a scene from "The Dead Zone" – a movie based on a Stephen King novel – but he diplomatically kept that to himself.

Lambert was not sleeping well. His nights were disturbed by unsettling dreams, which he couldn't recall when awake. He'd be at the pub until after 11pm and then had to be up at 5am to get to work and open the pumps at 6. The first part of his shift lasted until noon – then he'd go home and back to work at 6pm through to 10pm – then to the pub – and repeat – six days a week. Ewan plodded through this and his thoughts grew more and more fuzzy.

One day, when he was home alone in the afternoon, Lambert needed something from his bedroom. As he climbed the stairs, he noticed something lying on a step, about halfway up. Curiously, he picked it up. It was a small black and white picture – the kind you would get in a strip of four, from a Photobooth machine. With a shock, he realised what was on the picture. It was his wife, Lorraine. It must have been taken years ago, for she looked a lot younger than she did now. Ewan studied it closely. It was unmistakably her but how the fuck had it got here? He knew for a fact, he'd never seen it before in his life.

For the rest of that day and the following morning, Ewan puzzled over his mystery find. He considered that, perhaps Auntie Fiona had planted it, to come up with some theatrical revelation, but he had to discard that idea. She had never been to their home in Fife. How else could she have obtained it? He had never seen it before. He had no idea how it could have gotten to this house in Essex. It was as if someone was messing with his head. But who? Auntie Fiona was home the next day and Lambert broached the subject with her. She too was baffled – which convinced him, she had nothing to do with it. She did point out that the stairs had form for mysterious events. Not long before Ewan had come to stay, his cousin Jeff had claimed to have been attacked there by an unseen entity. It had thrown him down the stairs so violently that he'd pulled the banister handrail from the wall. Lambert later confirmed this story with Jeff – and he said it was true. He hadn't seen anything – but he'd felt hands on him. Ewan was skeptical but again, said nothing. He did wonder if Fiona's dabbling with Spiritualism had opened some kind of supernatural portal – and the photograph had been manifested that way. Then he dismissed that as too far-fetched. It would just have to remain a mystery.

It was two days later that the next incident occurred. Lambert's nights were becoming more disturbed and the dreams more graphic. He was even able to remember snatches of them. There was blood, fire and violence – and that troubled him greatly. He had never been a violent man – but the ferocity of the dreams was somehow appealing to something inside him. Ewan felt conflicted and on the edge. Then, he was alone in the house, once again. There was a downstairs loo – just a w.c. – the main bathroom being upstairs. It was just outside the back door, in a kind of workshop affair. Ewan went in to void his bowels and as he sat there, he became aware of noises outside the door. It seemed to be multiple voices, whispering. Lambert couldn't decipher what they were saying, as they didn't speak in unison, but talked over each other.

He did fancy that he heard some familiar names – but that might just be imagination.

Much as he hurried, it still took a couple of minutes for him to finish up and get out. There was no-one there. He re-entered the house through the back door and into the kitchen. There, on the kitchen wall, written in what looked like blood, were three names – Glynis Mc Mullan, Sheena Melville and Lorraine Lambert. Beneath them was the depiction of a dagger and three words – "Kill Them All". Lambert was totally spooked and his knees almost gave way. These were the three women that he blamed for his downfall. How could this be happening? He staggered through to the living room and collapsed on the couch. That's where Auntie Fiona found him, when she came home, twenty minutes later. She immediately saw that something was wrong. Wordlessly, Lambert took her through to the kitchen. He half expected the writing to be gone – but it wasn't.

Fiona was in her element – a spooky mystery to get involved in. Lambert was not suspicious of her. Two of the names written on the wall, she would have had no way of knowing. Over the next couple of hours, Ewan pulled himself together enough to go and do his evening shift – but he was deeply troubled. He didn't go to the pub that night, but hurried home to speak to his auntie. She'd been busy. There was a sub-section of her Spiritualist group who specialized in investigating hauntings. They called themselves "Ghostbusters" – no doubt aiming for irony. A couple of them were coming in the afternoon tomorrow, to interview Ewan and examine the writing on the wall. He was happy enough at this but wasn't sure just how they could actually help.

Ewan went to bed, but sleep wouldn't come. His mind was too active and he kind of feared the dreams that might materialise. For a long time, he tossed and turned, but eventually he did drop off. Suddenly, he awoke, in a panic. Someone, or something was pinning him to the bed. It was dark and he couldn't see his assailant but it felt like someone was kneeling on his chest. He couldn't breathe. He tried to cry out for help, but couldn't utter a sound. Much as he struggled, Ewan couldn't shift his phantom attacker. Then, as suddenly as it had started, it stopped. Lambert sat up, in a cold sweat. Relief flooded over him, as he realised he'd been dreaming. He swung his legs over the edge of the bed and turned on his bedside lamp. He was still shook up. Ewan reached for his cigarettes on the bedside table. Suddenly and violently, he was attacked again. Lambert was thrown back on the bed and was once more pinned down. There was no doubt this time that he was awake. Despite the light being on,

Ewan still couldn't see the assailant. He sensed, rather than saw, something looming over him. Then, inches away from his face, a malevolent voice snarled – "KILL THEM ALL!" Message delivered, the entity abruptly departed, leaving Lambert traumatized and shaking.

Ewan slept no more that night. He sat up with the lights on and chain-smoked whilst drinking from a bottle of Grouse that he kept in the room. There wasn't much whisky left in the bottle by the time daylight came. Ewan was wrecked – but strangely, didn't feel drunk. He was dislocated and sleep-deprived, not to mention highly disturbed – but his mind seemed to be working overtime. Even awake, he was seeing flashes of blood-soaked violence. It was as if he wasn't in control of his own mental functions. Needless to say, he did not go to work that morning. When he finally pulled himself together enough to leave his room and go downstairs, he tearfully poured out his heart to Auntie Fiona. She listened sympathetically and then phoned Ewan's boss, to say that he was ill. His boss was not happy and said if Ewan didn't come in for his evening shift, then he wasn't to bother coming in at all.

Fiona managed to calm Ewan somewhat and reassured him that the Ghostbusters would find a way to help. Maybe an exorcism would be the answer. Lambert was still in a dark place, without much confidence that anyone could help – but he did calm down enough to eat some breakfast and drink some tea. The television was on, more as background than anything else. No-one was actually watching it, as such. Suddenly, the picture zoomed into an extreme close-up of the female presenter's face. "KILL THEM ALL!" she snarled – and then the scene reverted to normal. Shocked, Lambert looked at Fiona, but she didn't seem to have seen anything unusual. The message had, apparently, been only for him.

A plan was formulating in Lambert's mind – one that he did not wish to share. Patiently he waited for the Ghostbusters arrival. He'd have to get that out of the way, before he could do anything. At about 2pm, they arrived. The Ghostbuster's representatives were a young man and an equally young woman. They were very earnest in their approach. They sat and listened attentively, taking notes, as Ewan recounted his story. Then, they went to the kitchen, to see the ominous writing on the wall. There was some debate, as to whether it was blood or paint. Now that it had time to dry, the conclusion was that it was probably paint.

The young man, Tony by name, suggested it might be an idea, if Fiona employed her skills as a trance-medium, to see if anything made itself known. Given the attack on Ewan in his bedroom, that might be the best place to do it. He would accompany Fiona and record it on a small portable cassette recorder he had brought along. Meanwhile, the young woman, Anna, would interview Lambert a bit further. Anna was quite thorough in her questioning. She wanted to know the story behind the names that had been written on the wall. Ewan was quite evasive. He was growing tired of this approach. He had made his mind up on what he had to do – and had preparations to make.

Tony and Auntie Fiona returned downstairs. Their efforts had apparently been fruitless. Nothing had happened. As the Ghostbusters finished up their investigation, Tony replayed the tape he'd made upstairs. At first, there were only two voices on the recording – Fiona and Tony conversing – but when she went into her trance, a third voice appeared. Neither of them had heard anything at the time. The voice was low and sibilant – and its words indistinct – so much so, that no-one could make out what it was saying. No-one that is, except Ewan. He heard it clear – "KILL THEM ALL". The Ghostbusters departed, with Tony promising to try and enhance the tape and find out what had been said on it. Ewan didn't care. He already knew – but kept it to himself.

After their visitors had left, Ewan told his Auntie that he was going upstairs for a little nap before he went to work. He said he was feeling better and she believed him. Upstairs, Lambert went into his cousin Jeff's room. Jeff liked clasp-knives. He had quite a large collection of them, which he kept in his room. Lambert selected two of them – one with a thin blade and another with a broad one. He had no particular reason for his choices. They just felt right. A couple of hours later, Ewan put on the boiler suit, with the garage's name on the front, that he wore to work. In one pocket he had the two knives and in another, the stash of cash that he'd accumulated over the last couple of months. It was a fair amount, given the hours he worked. There wasn't a lot of opportunity to spend much.

Lambert said his goodbyes to his Aunt and Uncle and set off, ostensibly for work. Of course, he had no intention of going there. His destination lay hundreds of miles north – in Fife. Lambert's mind was remarkably clear. Given his lack of sleep, he shouldn't be feeling this lucid – but now he was committed to a course of action – the right course of action – he was at ease. Lambert drove all through the night, stopping only once for petrol. The car he was in belonged to his cousin who was looking to sell it. It was a souped up red Ford

Capri with a black vinyl roof. Jeff had loaned it to him, for getting back and forth to work, until he found a buyer. It was a fast vehicle and gobbled up the miles rapidly.

At just before five in the morning, Lambert approached the town of Methil. It was daylight but still early enough that most people would still be abed. He was motoring along quite quickly when he saw two crows ahead of him, feasting on some roadkill. They both flapped into the air as he bore down on them – but one was a bit too slow. It hit his windscreen with a resounding thwack and a deal of blood spatter. Lambert slammed on the brakes. He was shocked and upset at just having killed a living thing. The sight of the blood on the windscreen sickened him and suddenly he had a moment of clarity. Such a small death had triggered pity in him and yet he was embarked on a monstrous mission to shed human blood. While he was depressed and vulnerable, something malevolent had latched onto him and was manipulating his thoughts. Either that, or he was having a psychotic breakdown. He got out of the car and lit a cigarette. It was time to consider. The crow was lying in an untidy bundle of black feathers. Apparently it wasn't yet dead, for it turned its head towards him and called three times. Anyone else would just have heard – caw – caw – caw – but Lambert heard what it was really saying – "KILL THEM ALL". And with that, he was drawn back in and all hope of redemption was gone.

Five minutes later, Lambert parked outside the semi-detached house that Glynis Mc Mullan shared with her grandmother. Glynis was the hysterical bitch, with a paranoid imagination, who had started his troubles. She'd misinterpreted what had happened that late afternoon and then embroidered her story to make it worse. He'd given her a lift home once, so was aware where she lived. It was still early and Lambert knew the occupants were still asleep – just like he knew to go round to the backdoor. The guiding voice in his head told him so.

Lambert walked up the garden path and made his way to the backdoor. He tried the handle but it was locked. As he stood there, he heard the lock mechanism turning. When he pushed the handle down this time, the door swung open and he entered the kitchen. Lambert stood for a moment. The house was absolutely silent, apart from the ticking of the kitchen clock. It was one of those old-fashioned ones with a pendulum. Quickly, Lambert undressed, until he was completely naked. Then, taking the thin-bladed knife, he moved through the kitchen, the hallway and up the stairs. Ewan knew which bedroom to go to first.

The grandmother was asleep, lying on her right side. Lambert moved stealthily to the bed. In one fluid movement, he clamped his left hand over the woman's mouth and slid the knife home at the base of her skull. She died instantly. Lambert withdrew the blade and a little blood dribbled from the wound – surprisingly little. When he'd killed the crow, a little earlier, Lambert had felt pity. Now he just felt horny. Who knew, killing could be erotic? His erection preceded him as he left that room and went to Glynis's.

She too was asleep as Lambert entered her bedroom. He stood for a couple of minutes watching her and savouring what lay ahead. Then he padded silently, to stand over her. Once again he clamped his hand over the woman's mouth. She came awake, eyes wide with fright. Lambert held the knife up in front of those terrified eyes. "Remember me?" he asked. "Now listen to me carefully. Your grandmother is tied up and gagged in the next room. I'm going to take my hand away. If you make a sound, I'll kill you and then go and kill her too. Understand? The frightened woman nodded. Lambert took his hand away from her mouth and used it to pull the bedclothes off and throw them on the floor. Glynis gave a little gasp and Lambert snarled, "Quiet!"

The woman whimpered a little but otherwise held her peace. She was wearing a longish white tee-shirt as a nightdress. Lambert ran his eyes over her. Glynis was a good-looking young woman in her mid-twenties, with shoulder length brown hair. Lambert had always fancied her. "Lose the tee-shirt – quickly!" he ordered. The woman scrambled to comply. She couldn't have failed to notice his hard-on and must have known what lay in store. Lambert ran his eyes over her naked body. It was everything he'd expected. He was loving this – loving the feeling of power. "You see," Lambert said. "If I'd wanted to rape you that day, I would have done it. I only locked the front doors because we were going into my office to talk. There's a lot of expensive equipment in the building and everyone else had gone home. Anyone could have come in and stolen anything. Whenever you asked, I unlocked the doors and let you out. I never laid a finger on you – yet you still went to the cops. You lied and exaggerated. The allegations you made, ended my marriage and career. Now it's payback time."

Glynis tried to plead but Lambert ordered her to silence and threatened her with the knife. She subsided and waited in apprehension for whatever was about to happen. Lambert climbed onto the bed holding the knife to the side of the woman's neck. He gave it a little prick, drawing blood, just to remind her it was there. With his left hand he positioned his cock and then drove it hard into her. It was tight and dry, but that was alright. He knew it would be hurting her and that suited him just fine. "Is this what you were afraid of that day? Lambert asked as he pounded into her. "See – if you had just left things alone – this wouldn't be happening. It didn't happen then but it's happening now – because of your lies."

Lambert was super excited but he held his climax back. He didn't want this to finish too soon. He wanted Glynis to suffer and he wanted her to have plenty of time to think about what was happening. She was whimpering and gasping with pain – and this spurred Lambert on to greater brutality. He lost track of time, enraptured by his overweening sense of power. This was revenge – and it was sweet. At last, Lambert decided it was time. As he climaxed, he drove the blade into Glynis's neck. There was a moment of synergy between them. As he spasmed in orgasm, she spasmed in death. As he pumped semen into her, she pumped blood over his hand. It was the most magnificent and mind-blowing orgasm Lambert had ever had. Spent, he collapsed on top of her, feeling euphoric. It had all gone perfectly. Gratefully, Lambert kissed the dead woman's lips.

There was no time to bask in the afterglow. That was one down, but there were still two to go. Lambert went to the bathroom and washed himself clean of Glynis's blood. He examined himself in the mirror to check that he was clean. He had rinsed the knife too and dried it thoroughly, before folding the blade back into the handle. Then Lambert went downstairs to the kitchen and got dressed. Suddenly he was hungry. Going to the fridge, he found some cheese and made himself a sandwich. There was no rush now. His next target, Sheena Melville, lived some distance away in Falkirk. He couldn't get there in time to catch her before she went to work, so he intended to be waiting for her when she got home in the afternoon. His wife, Lorraine, was only a few miles away, in Kirkcaldy – but he was saving her for last. He wanted the bodies to be discovered, so that Lorraine would know he was coming for her.

Lambert exited the house and got into his car. He took his time driving to Falkirk. His only worry was that his Auntie Fiona might join the dots – the portentous writing on the kitchen wall coupled with Lambert's own disappearance – and perhaps inform the police but then he dismissed that thought. It was unlikely. Sheena Melville was older than Lambert. She was a former workmate and lover of his. That fateful afternoon, when he had unwittingly scared Glynis, he was speaking to her on Sheena's behalf. She was looking for a suitable younger woman to help her with a project she was planning. When the shit had hit the fan, she could have spoken up in Lambert's defence, but because her husband was suspicious of her relationship with him, she was afraid of getting involved and had thrown him under the bus. Well – she'd live to regret that.

Lambert reached Sheena's home, late in the morning. When he'd got dressed after dealing with Glynis, he hadn't put on his garage boiler suit – so he was in his ordinary clothes. He reckoned they would attract less attention in Sheena's refined neighbourhood. She lived in a fairly large bungalow, set amongst similar. Her husband mostly worked away from home and her youngest daughter, who still lived with them, would be at school. The chances were, that the house would be empty. Lambert parked his Capri in the next street and walked to the bungalow. As he neared it, his senses told him he had been right. The house was empty. On this mission, locks did not seem to be a problem. As Lambert neared the door, he heard them disengage.

Lambert made himself comfortable in Sheena's home. There were hours to kill before anyone got home. He switched on the tv and fetched a bottle of whisky and a glass from the drinks cabinet. Yes – she had a drinks cabinet. He settled down to drink and watch tv. The news channel was of particular interest. He wanted to see if the bodies had been discovered in Fife. Lambert figured that the murders were gruesome enough, that they would definitely feature on the news. There was no mention, the whole time he watched. Late in the afternoon, Lambert's inner voice warned him someone was coming. He went quickly to the window and looked out. It was Sheena's daughter, Jackie, coming home from school. Lambert couldn't remember if she was fourteen or fifteen. She was a pretty, blond girl, with lovely blue eyes and had always been pleasant and friendly to Lambert. He liked her.

Lambert had both knives with him. He selected the one with the broader blade. It looked more frightening, he considered, and he didn't want to hurt Jackie – he just wanted to scare her into compliance. There was only one door into the house, which opened into a hallway. Lambert went and stood against the wall at the side of the living room door and waited. He heard the girl come in and walk up the hall. She must have been going first to her own room, because she walked past the doorway where Lambert was standing. Swiftly and silently, he stepped out and grabbed her from behind. He put his hand over her mouth to stifle the scream that almost escaped the startled girl. "Stay calm, Jackie," he told her, in what he hoped was a soothing voice. "It's me – Ewan – your Mum's friend. I'm not going to hurt you. Just do what I tell you and everything will be fine."

Lambert held the knife up in front of Jackie's face, so that she understood the consequences of disobedience. Then he maneuvered her back into the living room and guided her over to the armchair he had been using previously. He sat down and pulled Jackie down onto his lap.

"Now – we're going to sit here quietly until your Mum comes home. I just want to talk to her. Don't say a word. No questions. I'm going to take my hand off your mouth now. One sound – and I'll have to cut you."

Lambert knew that the girl was frightened – and he found that quite arousing. She was a cute little thing, dressed in her blue school blazer and grey skirt. She smelled nice. Although Jackie was still at school, she wasn't really a little girl, Lambert reasoned. He'd noticed the swell of her breasts beneath her school blouse. She was young and fresh and he had a hard-on. It was pressing against the girl's bottom and she had to be aware of it. "What the hell," Lambert thought. "Consequences didn't matter now," He used his left hand to open a couple of buttons on Jackie's blouse. Then he slid his hand in and up inside her bra, to fondle her right tit. She stiffened and drew in a shocked breath, but said nothing. Fear precluded speech. Lambert tweaked her nipple and felt it stiffen. This pleased him a lot. He considered having her, there and then on the floor – but Sheena would be home soon. If he was distracted, shagging the girl, his main target might be able to escape and fetch help. He would have to be patient. After he had dealt with the mother, then there'd be time to enjoy the daughter. He still did not intend to kill Jackie. She had done nothing to harm him. Still – Glynis's grandmother hadn't harmed him either – and he'd killed her. It was something to think on.

Lambert was so absorbed in his thinking and his pleasure in Jackie's breast, that the first he knew of Sheena's arrival was when the front door opened. He realised that the warning voice had been there but that he'd kind of tuned it out. That couldn't be good. Quickly he removed his hand from Jackie's blouse and grabbed a handful of her hair instead. He held the razor sharp blade of the knife hard against her throat and hissed a warning to be quiet. Sheena came directly into the living room and her eyes went wild with fright when she saw the scene before her. "Come in Sheena and close the door," Lambert told her. "Unless you want me to hurt your daughter." Sheena stood immobile for a moment or two. She was a petite woman with short grey hair and a pixie-like face. Then she turned and ran.

Lambert was surprised and immdiately furious. Sheena was obviously running for help and probably didn't believe he'd hurt Jackie. In the one movement, Lambert stood up, slashed Jackie's throat and threw her aside. He pounded after Sheena, his anger lending his feet wings. She'd only got as far as her driveway when he caught up with her. She was screaming blue murder and calling for help. Lambert crashed into her and bore her, face first, to the ground, knocking all the air from her lungs and silencing her. He was incandescent with rage. It had been his intention to spend time exacting his revenge upon her. There was no way he could risk that now. Roughly, he turned her over so that he could scream into her face. "You cowardly cunt. Your daughter's dead because you ran away – just like you always run away. In a frenzy, he began punching the knife into her body. He had no idea how many times he stabbed her. He wasn't counting. He continued long after life had fled Sheena's body. Then the voice in his head finally made itself heard. It was time to go.

Lambert got to his feet and ran. Neighbours had heard Sheena's screams and some were coming outside to see what had caused the commotion. Lambert's clothes were soaked with blood and it had splattered all over his face. His hand and the knife dripped red as he fled the scene. People on the pavement scattered at his approach and wisely so. If any had come within reach, the knife would have been plunged into them also. As he ran, Lambert had come to the decision that he was going to make a run, straight for Kirkcaldy. The alarm was obviously being raised right now, but it would take time for the police to arrive here and assess what had happened. With a bit of luck, he could be clear of Falkirk and across the Kincardine Bridge before any alerts were broadcast. Someone would get a description of his car and the licence number, but there was nothing he could do about that right now, but run.

Lambert hadn't gone far when he realised this plan was not going to work. His blood covered appearance was drawing attention from passing motorists and pedestrians as he drove past them. "Fuck Sheena – even dead, she was causing him hassle." He was feeling on the verge of a full-blown panic attack.

His link to whatever was guiding him, seemed to be growing more and more tenuous. The clarity of his mission was dissipating. Perhaps the words "Kill them all" didn't apply only to the three women named – but to all women. Was that what he was supposed to do? Maybe he should stop the car, get out and run amok on the streets – stabbing any woman he could get near and any man who tried to stop him.

Then, calmness and lucidity suddenly descended on Lambert. The voice in his head told him that all would be well – but he had to stay focussed. He had let himself become distracted while waiting for Sheena. His lustful interest in the daughter, had made him forget what his main task was. Taking his pleasures and causing collateral harm was fine – but he had to take care of his primary mission, above all else. Do that – and he would be fine. Lambert was now clear of the town. His first imperative was to ditch the Capri and get himself cleaned up. On his left, the entrance to a farm road was coming up. Lambert knew, with certainty, that he should take it.

Lambert drove along the farm track for about half a mile and came to a turn off – but he went past it. That wasn't where he was meant to go. He carried on the twisting, turning, single track road and finally, up ahead, he saw his destination. It was a stone-built farmhouse, in a cluster of out buildings, including a large, red-painted barn. Lambert stopped the car at the side of the barn, where it couldn't be seen from the house. Then he walked boldly to the front door, confident that no-one was looking out. His mentor told him so. Lambert knocked loudly on the door and stood back, the thin-bladed knife held behind his back. A few moments later, a stout-framed, middle-aged man opened the door. He was taken aback when he saw Lambert's blood soaked appearance. "I've had an accident," Lambert said. "Can I use your phone?" Before the farmer could reply, Lambert took one quick step forward and thrust the knife up under his chin. He withdrew the blade and stabbed twice more into the man's chest.

The farmer crumpled to the floor and a woman's voice called out, "Jim. Are you alright?" Lambert stepped over the dying man and went towards the voice. A worried looking woman came hurrying from the farmhouse interior and straight into Lambert. His knife swiftly ended her life too. Now he had work to do. Lambert moved the bodies to a space beneath the stairs, where they wouldn't be seen if anyone looked in the windows or through the letterbox. Then he drove the Capri into the barn and put it behind a stack of hay bales, before covering it with a tarpaulin. It wouldn't hide it from a proper search but the car wouldn't be immediately visible to a superficial look into the barn. Lambert went back to the house, got a mop and cleaned up the blood that had been spilled on the doorstep. Now, it was time to sort himself out.

Lambert went to the bathroom and stripped off. He ran a bath and got in. When he was certain that all traces of blood had been washed away, Lambert got out, dried himself and went to look in the mirror. What he saw there shocked him. He wouldn't have recognised himself. His face was pale and haggard with large black circles around his eyes. The eyes themselves, were so bloodshot that they almost looked to actually be red. His lower face was covered in a grubby stubble. He wasn't looking good. Then the face in the mirror began to talk. Lambert put a hand to his mouth to check that he wasn't doing this himself. But the mirror face was speaking independently of his actual face.

"It's not too late," the mirror face told him. "You can end this, Ewan. There's a shotgun in a gun safe. Get it and blow your head off. What you're doing is evil. You justify it to yourself, by thinking you are possessed and being forced to do things against your nature. That isn't true. You are indeed possessed, but the entity possessing you is only enabling you to do exactly what you want to do. It is in alignment with your true nature – otherwise you could have fought it. The rest of your life is numbered in mere hours – believe me, I know. End it now – before you do even more malicious evil. You know it's the right thing." Lambert continued to stare into the mirror and realised that whatever he'd been seeing was gone. The face in the mirror now, was merely his reflection. "Fuck you," he said. "But thanks for telling me about the shotgun. That'll come in handy."

Lambert went to the farmer's bedroom and rummaged through a clothes closet. He got dressed. The clothing didn't fit him well. It hung loosely on him, but he wasn't going to a fashion show. As long as the clothes didn't attract undue attention, that's all that was required. Pausing only to fetch the gun and a box of ammunition, Lambert took the keys for the Range Rover that was parked in the farmyard and left the house. With this vehicle, he should be able to get to Kirkcaldy, without being detected and stopped by the cops. It was time to complete his mission.

Lambert's wife, Lorraine had hurt him deeply. He had been contented in his job, but she was unsettled and wanted to move back to he native Lanarkshire. So, at her instigation, he'd got a job in that area. He had just completed his notice period at his old job, but had not yet taken up his new post, when the complaint was made against him. His old employers informed his new ones and they promptly withdrew the job offer. Lambert was left unemployed, with little prospect of obtaining work in the same field. His reputation had been fatally tainted. Lambert approached his Union for help, but they proved worse than useless. At first, Lorraine had been supportive but as time passed, she grew less so. She persuaded Lambert to go away for a few days, so that they could both think things over. They were then to meet up and talk things over. It was all a ruse. Lorraine had used the time to alter the lease with the housing association they rented from, so that she was the sole tenant – and then she'd had the locks changed. Lambert was no longer welcome and was told to leave. They had a daughter, less than two years old and Lorraine had three other kids, that had treated Lambert as their father. That had all been taken away from him. Lorraine was indeed worthy of retribution.

Nothing mattered to Lambert now but completing his mission. He was unafraid of consequences, because he didn't believe there would be any. He believed what the face in the mirror had told him. Soon, he would be dead. As long as Lorraine died first, that would be fine. Lambert drove carefully, not wishing to draw any police attention to himself. He reached Kirkcaldy without incident and was soon nearing the district where his former marital home was situated. He was excited. Soon, all his persecutors would be paid back. The end was in sight. Then, his stomach dropped. Two police cars were coming up fast behind him, blue lights flashing and sirens going. Had he been discovered? He began formulating his response – but it proved unnecessary. The cars overtook him and went speeding past.

Lambert knew, and his internal voice confirmed, that the cops were on their way to his former home. They had either found Glynis's body and worked out a link between that, Sheena and himself – or Auntie Fiona had had a revelation and got in touch with them with a warning. She did, after all, have the three names written on her kitchen wall – with the instruction to "KILL THEM ALL." Whatever the case, they were on their way to protect Lorraine. Lambert was on the verge of panic but his inner voice calmed him. The police would move his wife and the kids somewhere they considered safe. They would think that there was no way for him to discover that location – so actual security would be minimal. He just had to wait, be patient and his guide would lead him to her.

Feeling much happier, Lambert drove past the entrance to the entrance to his wife's street and headed for a nearby supermarket carpark. He would wait there, until the time came. He was out of cigarettes, so he went into the shop to get some more. Smoking would help him to pass the time – and a lot of time did pass. It was over four hours later and darkness had fallen when he became aware where he had to go. It wasn't a police station, as he had feared, but a house on the other side of the town. There were two police officers with the family – a man and a woman – but that wasn't a problem. Lambert did have the shotgun, after all. He started the car and set off to complete his final task.

It was only a fifteen minute drive, to get to his destination. Lambert knew that police resources were concentrated on the empty marital home. They were lying in wait, hoping to ambush him. Well, they would be disappointed. He drove past the terraced house and saw that all the curtains were drawn but there were lights on both upstairs and down. He did hope the kids were in bed, because he didn't want to harm them – but, unfortunately, collateral casualties sometimes happened. Lambert stopped the car about fifty yards past the house and readied himself. He had no experience with guns but the operation of the shotgun looked straightforward enough It was double-barrelled, with two triggers. He broke it open and inserted a couple of cartridges, putting a handful of spares into his pockets. It was time.

Lambert got out of the car. He held the shotgun down by his side, to make it less conspicuous. He'd only taken a couple of steps when something hit him hard. He staggered and almost fell down. He realised it hadn't been anything physical but something psychic in nature. Suddenly he was alone. His inner voice was gone. His mentor was no longer with him. Panic rose within Lambert. Almost he decided to get back in the Range Rover and drive away – but he tried to master his fear. The house was right there. Just get the job done. Maybe this was a test. Pass it and his guide would return. The cops in the house wouldn't be armed. He could easily blow them away. Nevertheless, he needed a moment to get himself under control. His stomach was knotted and his heart was pounding. Lambert walked back to the Range Rover and placed the shotgun on its roof. He leaned against the car and lit a cigarette, his shaking hands rendering this simple task difficult. When that one was finished, he still wasn't ready – so he lit another – finding it easier this time. By the time he'd finished his second smoke, Lambert's panic attack had subsided enough for him to continue. He picked up the gun and began walking.

When Lambert got to the front door, it was, of course locked. Without his guide, this was a problem – but he had a shotgun. In so many movies, he'd seen people shooting their way through locks. He could blow the door open and still reload before the cops could do anything. Lambert took a step back and raised the gun to his shoulder. As he did so he became aware of approaching sirens. Someone in the house must have seen him or some nosey neighbour had noticed the gun on the car's roof and called the police. No time to waste. Lambert aimed at the lock and pulled both triggers. The recoil shocked him. He was knocked a couple of steps backwards and had a numbing pain in his right shoulder. It took him much longer than he'd anticipated, as he fumbled to eject the spent cartridges and insert fresh ones.

Lambert snapped the gun shut, stepped forward and kicked the door with the sole of his foot. He had expected it to burst open but the door did not yield. What the fuck? What had he done wrong? It worked every time in the movies. Could be the door was reinforced. His brain wasn't functioning properly. He was confused. What to do now? He thought and thought but the only thing he came up to was to try again. Lambert raised the shotgun once more to his bruised shoulder. As he did so, he became aware of a blue strobing light and someone shouting at him to drop his gun. Well that wasn't going to happen. The cavalry had obviously arrived.

Lambert turned to face the newcomers. There were two police cars slewed across the road and a third one approaching fast. Four figures couched for shelter behind the stopped cars and he could see that at least two of them held handguns. He had to take out the firearms officers before he mopped up the rest. With the shotgun at his shoulder, Lambert sighted along the barrel and took a couple of steps forward. He saw some flashes and then was punched multiple times in the chest.

****

When the ritual was over, Auntie Fiona was sure they'd been successful. All day, she'd been sending healing energy to Ewan. At times she had felt close to making a connection with him but it had always broken down. As well as being his Aunt, she was also his Godmother. She felt a powerful obligation to help him. Given her strong familial and spiritual relationship to Ewan, the "Ghostbusters" – all five of them, this time – had suggested trying a remote exorcism. These were unusual but not unheard of. They had just completed it and Fiona was optimistic. She was sure she had felt something shifting at the climax of the ritual. Hopefully they'd helped Ewan before he did anything he couldn't come back from.

****

As Ewan Lambert died, he wished that in the afterlife, he could help someone, as he'd been helped — that he could possess a living person to complete the task in which he had failed. It was his only hope.

The Ghost of Riverside Day Centre.

All the other stories in this collection are fiction but this final one is true and happened to me. In the mid-1970s, I worked at a place in Stirling, called Riverside Day Centre. It was a small facility for physically disabled adults – and it had a ghost that didn't like me. For five days a week, Monday to Friday, we catered for people with a variety of disabilities – many in wheelchairs. At the Centre they would take part in activities and crafts, such as woodwork, leather working, candle-making, batik and screen-printing. Apart from this there was companionship and social interaction for the clients and much needed respite for families and spouses. It gave them time to themselves, knowing that their disabled relatives were being looked after.

The place was in some turmoil when I started working there. A much loved manager left for pastures new – and it took some time to replace him. Of the two other full-time members of staff, one was away on a year's training course and the other went on maternity leave. I'd been coming to the Centre in a voluntary capacity. My uncle was the driver/handyman and he had suggested to the manager that I might be able to help. There was a young lad, who had suffered brain damage as the result of a cycling accident. He needed something to improve his concentration. He was keen on learning to play guitar and the manager thought this was the very thing he'd need. I was out of work at the time and I played guitar. So I was conscripted as a volunteer. For a few months, I worked in that capacity, including going on a Centre holiday to Belgium. When the staff member left to go on the training course, I got temporary employment to replace her. Less than a month into this job, the others left as I described earlier. It meant that I was left in charge, with only a care-assistant and three or four volunteers to help me. There was ancillary staff – a cook, drivers and escorts for the mini-buses, but they weren't involved directly with the clients and their activities. It was hectic and shambolic, but we kept it going. That's the background to my story.

One Saturday, I'd gone into the Centre to make a customized belt for a young woman who used to be one of our clients. She'd moved to a different Centre and they didn't do leather work so she asked me to make her one with the words, "Shakin' Stevens" embossed on it. Obviously, she was a fan. I was alone in the building as I cut the leather strip from the hide and attached a buckle to it. Each letter had to be stamped individually on the belt. By the time I started doing this, it was about lunchtime and I was feeling peckish. I went to the kitchen to make myself a snack. The Centre was housed in large huts, that had once been annexe classrooms for Riverside School. The office, kitchen and dining area were in one hut, that sat parallel to Edward Street. These had been connected to two other huts, forming a U shaped complex. One held the craft area and the other the workshop, where I'd been working on the belt. A passageway connected this to the kitchen.

As I made myself a cheese sandwich, I heard footsteps coming up this passage, from the direction of the workshop. They were very distinctive. There'd be the sound of a step followed by the sound of the other foot being dragged along the floor. One of our clients, Peter, walked with just such a gait. I wondered what the hell he was doing in on a Saturday and how he'd got past me without me seeing him. I walked to the kitchen door and popped my head out. The passageway was empty. Puzzled, I went down to the workshop to see if I'd been mistaken and that Peter had actually been going in the other direction. It too was empty. Still puzzled, but not particularly worried, I returned to the kitchen to finish and eat my sandwich.

After lunch, I returned to the workshop to finish the belt. There were two lines of three workbenches, set up with vices etc. for woodwork. I was working at the bench nearest the door. I carried on, absorbed in the job and looked up, just in time to see a tin can filled with paint brushes, suddenly hurtle from a bench at the bottom of the room. A few seconds later, a screwdriver did the same from the next bench up. Spooked, I decided it was time to go. I'd finish the belt on Monday, when there'd be other people around. When Monday came, the whole episode was still playing on my mind. I told my uncle about it. He said that the footsteps sounded like the way Annie (not her real name) had walked.

Annie had been a client at the Centre, before I got involved with it. One of the things the Centre did, was take the clients away on group holidays from time to time. As well as being a holiday for the clients, it gave their families a break also. The summer before I went to work at Riverside, Annie had gone on one such holiday, to somewhere in England. She hadn't really wanted to go but pressure had been put on her and she'd eventually agreed. Annie had the reputation of being quite an awkward and prickly lady. She resented being kind of forced to go away with the others – and probably rightly so. Anyway, as I've been told, she spent the holiday moaning, bitching and being nasty to all and sundry – and then she died, a day before they were due to come home. Now if I was a ghost, I'd be a bitter one under those circumstances – not that there had been any sign of her up to now. If it had been Annie that spooked me, then I was the first one she had manifested to. It made little sense. I hadn't been anywhere near the Centre when Annie was there.

In the next couple of weeks, Annie worked up a new trick. I called her Annie, though I'd no proof that it had anything to do with her. I imagined a bitter spirit, intent on wreaking vengeance on the living. Why she'd have a grudge with me, I didn't have any idea. I still don't. Anyway, I had cause to visit the Centre a couple of times after hours. Whenever I approached the double front doors, they would suddenly rattle, rather violently. It only happened after dark and when there was no-one already inside the building. Why this was so, I have no idea. Maybe Annie was flexing her ghostly muscles – trying out to see what she could achieve. Maybe she was trying to scare me. I fully admit that I was spooked, when it first happened – but I refused to be intimidated – especially by something so ethereal. At least at first, there was no creepy follow up to the eerie door rattling, when I went inside the building. I began to be quite blasé about it.

Late one Saturday night, I'd been drinking and watching movies on the telly, when the Police came to my door. The burglar alarm at the Centre had been triggered. I was down as the primary key-holders and thus they'd come to inform me and to accompany me to the building. As I'd been drinking, they drove me there, rather than following me in my own car. We got to the Centre and the alarm was blaring out and strobe lights were flashing inside. As the key-holder, I had to go first and unlock the doors. As we approached them, the doors did their customary forceful clattering. The two cops nearly shit themselves. They fell further back behind me – but I just smiled knowingly and carried on.

We got inside and I turned off the alarm. Accompanied by the two jumpy constables, I checked out the whole building. There was no-one there and no sign of a break in. It was impossible to say what had set off the alarm. It could have simply been a glitch or something had triggered the motion sensors. It was clear that there hadn't been an intruder. Satisfied, the Police departed and I was alone. I couldn't just lock up and leave. The alarm had to be reset. This entailed me calling into the company and waiting for an engineer to come and attend to it. There was nothing for me to do but wait. I sat in the office smoking and bored out of my mind. I hadn't thought to even bring a book with me to pass the time. It was a couple of hours before the engineer turned up – but it seemed a lot longer.

The engineer was very efficient and was in and out within fifteen minutes. By the time he was gone, the rain was pissing down. I was tired and on a come down from the alcohol I'd swallowed earlier. I couldn't face the thought of trudging home and getting soaked in the process. It's not as if Annie had done anything else to spook me. I decided to sleep the rest of the night in the Centre. There was a little room – The Therapy Room. It was small and contained only a sink, a chair and a therapy couch. That's where I chose to spend what was left of the night. The couch would serve fine as a bed. So, I locked the doors and made my way there. Despite my earlier nonchalance, I found it hard to get to sleep. The eerie goings on, despite their fairly innocuous nature, had made me uneasy. Annie had spooked me, more than I'd admitted to myself. I refused to let myself be chased however. So, somewhat illogically, I got up from the couch and locked the door with the internal thumb lock. Since when did a locked door ever deter a ghost? I settled down again, but left the light on. I drifted off and had a peaceful night – at least until morning. When I awoke, the light was off and the door stood wide open.

That took me a little while to come to terms with but time passed with no further ghostly shenanigans. On reflection, I suspect that Annie was building her psychic energy, ready for a more spectacular manifestation. I was conducting an illicit affair and needed a venue for an amorous liaison. The only premises I had access to was the Centre and it seemed ideal for my purposes. My lady friend and I used the Centre a couple of times, with no problems whatsoever – apart from the continued door rattling – which I simply ignored. There was a foam filled couch kind of thing and it was ideal for our activities.

It was on our third tryst that Annie took a hand. We were well advanced in our erotic endeavours and thoroughly engrossed in each other. Suddenly, it grew markedly colder. Startled we looked round and there, standing just a few feet away, was the figure of a woman. She was watching us intently. Her features were indistinct but there was no doubt that this was the figure of a woman. We both saw her clearly. It was most definitely not a trick of the light. Needless to say, we had paused in our activity. There's nothing like a ghostly apparition to cool your ardour. I don't know how long we lay there, under the scrutiny of this silent wraith. It was probably less than half a minute, but it seemed a lot longer. Then, the figure seemed to just dissolve and the temperature reverted to normal. We quickly got dressed and left.

I used this experience for an incident in one of my books (Koldunya – The Coven part one). I adapted it somewhat to fit the narrative I was constructing but the actual occurrence was much more scary than the one in the book, where only the woman sees the apparition and the man is skeptical.

I made a point of avoiding the Centre after dark, following that incident. One night, however, I had no choice. It was late in December and we were out for a pre-Christmas party at the local Rugby Club. All the clients were there and the Centre staff provided transport. This was in the shape of a mini-bus which broke down, just when it was time to take everyone home. There was another mini-bus parked at the Centre and I quickly made my way there. I had to go inside to get the keys. I'll always remember how violently the doors rattled that night. It was a lot more lively than any previous time. Chastened, I took a deep breath and got in and out again as quickly as possible.

Nothing happened in the building and, with some relief, I got into the vehicle and started the engine. It was a yellow painted high-cab Ford Transit mini-bus. I began to drive out onto the road. Suddenly the temperature plummeted. I felt an even greater chill between my shoulder blades. I knew right away that Annie was behind me. Instinctively, I looked up at the rear-view mirror, which gave sight of the vehicles interior. She was there, right behind me. I could see her face clearly and it was contorted in rage. My eyes were locked on her and I stalled the vehicle's engine. Suddenly the mirror shattered – as did both external wing mirrors. Shards of glass rained down on me – but no injury occurred. Badly shaken, I was alone in the mini-bus.

I don't remember how we got everyone home that night. I think I was in shock. That was the last time I encountered Annie. Even the door-rattling never happened again. I don't know why she appeared in the first place and I don't know why she focused on me. I also don't know why she went away. Perhaps she'd achieved something personal, by finally really scaring me. Perhaps she used up all her supernatural juice in one final grand gesture. I guess it will all remain a mystery and no satisfactory explanation will ever be reached. Annie isn't the only paranormal entity I've encountered. There have been several others. None of which, I ever got to the bottom of. I speculated of course but was unable to wrap everything up and tie it in a neat little bow. To me, that is the way of the supernatural. Anyone who tells you that they know how it all works – and furnishes you with glib explanations, well, they're lying to you and probably to themselves.

Printed in Great Britain
by Amazon